Straight Outta DC Productions presents……

Queen of DC 4: The Book of Revelations
By K Sherrie

S0-CYG-599

This book is a work of fiction. Names, characters, dates, places and incidents are products of the author's imagination or are used fictitiously. Any resemblance to actual persons, events or locales living or dead is entirely coincidental.

Copyright © 2015 by K Sherrie

All rights reserved. No part of this book may be reproduced or transmitted in any form or by any means without written permission of the author.

Prologue

"I finally managed to fall asleep close to 5am. I woke up a little after 10 and was beyond pissed off. I overslept so that meant I would be stuck with my kids all day and while I loved their asses with all that I was, my mind was cluttered with this Jake B shit so I had no more patience left to deal with the bullshit of my clan. I threw on my robe and made my way downstairs and my house was quiet. Too quiet. I didn't understand that because my kids rose with the sun and when them motherfuckas was up, they let you KNOW their asses was up. I walked around for a minute and finally found Papi in the kitchen. He was sitting at the table reading the newspaper and eating a bowl of fruit loops. I didn't understand how the fuck he could be some calm, like we all weren't scheduled to die as early as today!"

Juan smiles at Keeli when he sees her standing in there watching him.
"Good morning."
"What's up? Where the kids at?"
"At camp. I dropped them off. Why don't you grab something to eat? You barely touched your dinner last night."
"Nah I'm good. Eating is like the furthest thing from my mind right now."
"Suit yourself." Juan says as he continues to eat his breakfast.

"Baby…" Keeli starts to express her thoughts. "Baby I was thinking, maybe we should just take the kids and move down to Panama for a while and…"

"What?" Juan asks in disbelief.

"I'm serious. Let's just take the kids and just go. I'll sell my business, QDC will be the first to go. Fuck I'll give them shits away. Let's just go please."

Juan looks at Keeli and takes in the look of fear on her face. He lets out an exhausted sigh. "Ke, is you really that scared?"

"Yes! This nigga that neither of us have ever laid eyes on wants to kill us and our kids. I can't let that shit happen!"

"Ke calm down. You getting yourself all worked up."

"This nigga threatened our fucking family Juan! How the fuck am I NOT supposed to be worked up!" Keeli snaps as she starts to cry.

"That's not what I'm saying. Look, go take a shower and get dressed. I want you to come take a ride with me."

"Take a ride with you… The fuck you think this nigga playing Juan?!" Juan jumps up and smacks the bowl of cereal he was eating off the table. "Shut the fuck up and just do it! Remember it was your simple hardheaded ass that go us the fuck in this shit in the first place!"

Keeli walks out the kitchen without saying another word for two reasons. Knowing that Juan was right and not knowing where her protesting taking a ride would take things between them. Once she gets dressed, her and Juan drive out to Newington Virginia. Juan drives onto the huge farm property with a newly built single family estate sitting in the middle of it. Juan drives up the long driveway and stops in front of the oversized double doors. He turns the truck off and looks over at Keeli. "Come on."

"Who house is this Juan?"

"Man just come the fuck on." Juan gets out of his Range Rover and Keeli follows suit. They walk up to the double doors without saying another word to each other. Juan rings the doorbell and waits. A minute later a man a little over 6 feet tall with skin the color of dark chocolate, green eyes and dread that hang down the middle of his back opens the door. He smiles at Juan and the two men exchange a familiar hug. He finally speaks in a thick Jamaican accent.

"Good ta see ya boy. I thought ya wasn't coming for a second dere. Come on in." The mansteps to the side and allows Juan and Keeli to enter the house before closing the door. He leads them down the foyer and into the huge sunken living room. The 3 of them take seat on the oversized custom sectional. The man picks up a blunt from the ashtray on the glass table and sparks it. He takes a deep pull and then passes it to Juan. "So what brings ya way out here to see me?"

"Oh yeah, let me introduce y'all before we get to that. Unc, this is my wife Keeli. And babe this is my uncle. His name is Bobby, but the streets call him Jake B."

****

We Are Family

"I damn near swallowed my tongue when he said that shit. All this time, the nigga who apparently wanted my head was at the head of my family. What type of sick, twisted shit was this nigga tryna pull? I didn't know if I was more angry, because he should have and could have told me this shit last night. Or scared. A part of me was scared because for all I knew the same man who stood before the world and God and promised to love, honor and protect me forever had just hand delivered me to the nigga who wanted nothing more than my brains on the floor. My heart was racing a mile a minute and my mind was racing twice that. I started wondering if our whole relationship and marriage had been some bullshit once he found out where I stood in these streets. But it didn't make sense. I didn't know which way was up at this point. It served me no good when I looked over and peeped the glock under a magazine on the coffee table. I didn't even have a real fucking burner on me. My trusty no nonsense D.E was at home in the stash box of my rover. I had a little ass .22 in my purse. That wasn't shit compared to that glock. My shit could've been blown all over the wall behind me before I even got that bullshit out of my bag.

Although I was sweating bullets on the inside, I remained cool as a fan on the outside. I figured fuck it, let the chips fall where they may. If it was truly my time to go wasn't shit I could do to stop it, so it was what it was. I had a good run. I lived a fabulous life. I made fucking history. I was the biggest female dealer DC had ever seen. I played the game and made it all the way to the end. So fuck it I was ready for whatever Sissy son and brother had in store for me."

"It's nice to finally meet ya girl." Bobby speaks with his thick Jamaican accent. "Sorry me not make it to the wedding, but ya know me work is never done."

"I completely understand." Keeli smiles as they lock eyes.

"Hey unc, wanna hear some funny shit. I brought her out here to meet you not so much on a social call. Somebody has my lovely wife thinking you want to kill her." Juan chuckles.

"Why would I want dat gal? Me hardly even know ya. What ya talkin bout?"

"I talked to Daye because I wanted to meet with you to see how we could squash whatever beef it is between you and I. And before I go any further, I am truly sorry about what happened to your daughter." Keeli says sincerely. "But my peoples and me had nothing to do with that and…"

"What daughter ya speak of?" Bobby asks, confused by Keeli statement. I only got four boys gal.

"This is Roc's dad baby." Juan chimes in while chuckling at how discombobulated Daye has managed to get Keeli.

"This is crazy. So you don't have a daughter that has a baby by Daye?"

"Fuck No!" Bobby's voice booms. "Even if me had a daughter, she no lay up with the likes of him. I kill dem both no questions asked."

"Now wait a damn minute. So if that's not your daughter that died, why did your peoples hit my spot?" Keeli asks, now reeling with anger.

"Three of my peoples died that night. Almost four."

"First, me don't know what ya talk bout. I don't deal in coke. I don't do no robberies, and most importantly, my people NEVER leave witnesses. Right nephew?" Bobby chuckles.

"Yes Sir." Juan chuckles.

"So this foul ass nigga been lying to me the whole time?" Keeli asks, more so to herself that anyone, still in disbelief that she allowed him to play her the way he did.

"This is why you shouldn't keep shit from me. This nigga is a nobody Keeli."

"So does he even work for you?" Keeli questions Bobby, growing angrier by the second.

"No. He buys his weed from me. Nothing more." Bobby clarifies.

"And he buys coke from me through Roc." Juan informs her.

"I don't believe this shit. So the whole time, it was his foul ass doing me dirty."

"Yep. And again, this is why you should've told me what the fuck you had going on out here in these streets. That nigga would've been disappeared."

"Don't worry. He about to be front and center as an example when I make his ass eat the clip. Extended." Keeli assures them.

"I like her nephew." Bobby smiles, impressed with Keeli.

"Yeah she's a fire cracker unk. But I got this."

"No No nephew. I will take care of it. He use my name in vain, he feels my wrath. You know how it goes."

"But unk listen…."

"No. We will consider this my wedding gift y'all. His little area is prime real estate from my understanding."

"It is." Keeli co-signs.

"Well now it's yours. Burn that shit to the ground if you like."

"Well damn. Thank you Uncle Bobby." Keeli walks over to him and hugs him causing him to blush.

"No problem. Just take care of my nephew."

"I always have." Keeli says while smiling at Juan.

"It felt like the weight of the world had just been lifted off my shoulders. Knowing that the fucking terrorist was on my side, a part of my family and I wasn't a target had me feeling like the bell of the ball. But every time my mind thought of how this grimy ass Negro had played me out. The feeling I got was indescribable. Him and his whole squad was probably kicking back laughing at my dumb ass, running around requesting meetings and shit with a nigga who didn't even know who the fuck I was. I really felt played and wanted to take action. But Uncle Bobby said he was handling shit and well he didn't strike me as the kind of motherfucka you go pulling rank with.

Juan and I chilled a bit, put a few in the air with Unk, had lunch then he gave us a tour of his property and I got to ride a horse. We finally left and picked up our kids and went home. Juan kept teasing me about how I was tripping out tryna buy us tickets for the first thing smoking out the country when I thought Uncle Bobby was after us. I could laugh then, but yeah before that meeting that shit was no laughing matter on my end.

Two days later, Uncle Bobby called me at home. We talked about nothing at all for about 10 minutes. The last thing he said was "Well I will let you go on and get ready to watch the news." I'm glad I wasn't no ole green bitch cause that subliminal would've gone right over my head. I turned on the 5' o clock news and every channel was covering the same story. Local drug kingpin Dayeland Willis McAuthor, along with his son, his mother and his sister and four members of his notorious crew were found hog tied and decapitated in his home. I stared at the screen like daaaaaamnnnn unk was not playing. That's when I checked the caller ID and realized Unk's call came from Jamaica. This nigga was swift as a motherfucka.

I had one whole week, a measly 7 days before my publishing company was scheduled to open but I wasn't anywhere near finished with my book. There was always some other shit popping off that had me pulled away from getting my legit shit in order. And with Daye ass losing his head literally, it didn't help me get any closer to getting out the game and flying right. My phone STAYED ringing off the hook since the minute the news broke that his ass was DEAD. Folks from my crew kept getting approached by the same niggas who sold his weak ass product for pocket change for fucking decades. They were now trying to drop their resumes in my inbox. Daye ass had hella real estate and some real live loyal niggas holding him down. Then again I wasn't sure if it was loyalty or fear that kept them niggas in check all that time.

Either way, I wasn't looking to expand my work force because well my team was loyal and spoiled as fuck. Niggas and bitches rocking with that crown was set for life. Bitches got paid time off in my camp. I took care of my folks. They earned that shit. Wasn't nobody nowhere handing out benefits on the block but me. Call me crazy but I valued my folks and like I said, I was set for life. I wasn't gonna shit on the folks who got out there and kept it that way on my behalf. I did do those Daye nuts holding ass niggas a solid. I sent word via Donna that I understood their plight, but I wasn't looking to take on any more permanent employees HOWEVER, I was willing to offer them a buy in. I was letting bricks go at 16.5 apiece and they could keep their blocks to move it on. Them niggas wasn't no fools. Two days later, Donna came to me with orders that needed to be filled and straight money. I fucked with everybody except the niggas from Daye's home team. I aint know how they was truly feeling and I wasn't about to put myself in a situation where some mad ass nigga be speaking to them niggas downtown. I was good on that shit.

At the beginning of July, I put my peoples back on the street because the coast was clear now. We aint have to worry about nothing but collecting money. We had the city on LOCK. Wasn't nobody tryna fuck with nothing but that crown stamp. Around the second week of July, me and Tia got called in for a meeting with the prosecutor. They were dropping the charges against me. Randi was refusing to testify against me etc etc etc. So they dropped it. I was glad about that because 2 weeks later, I went for my annual check up and Juan funky ass had did it to me again. I was 10 weeks pregnant with baby number 5 for both of us…. And 6 in the grand total. We sat down and discussed this long and hard because truth be told, having an abortion was the first thing that came to mind. We went back and forth for about a week and finally ended up deciding to keep shorty. Like Juan said, this baby could fuck around and be President or something. So we decided to keep shorty but we were in agreement that the minute shorty was born I was having my tubes tied, burned and clipped and his ass was gonna have THE BIG V. This was it for us.

On August 1, Me, Juan and our kids left DC and headed to Miami. We decided to spend the entire month there. Roc came along with his new girl Deja. Him and the bitch Niyah split up a month after she had the baby. Shorty was black as shit and her and Roc BOTH were red…. You do the math cause I damn sure did. Randi came to me the day before we left and let me know that she had found a place out in Colorado but she couldn't move in until the first of December. She was so shook since I knew her little secret. But I was in good spirits. Everything was on a high note for me. So I shocked the shit out of her when I went back on my word and told her she didn't have to leave. I was trying something new…. It was called being nice. I was just praying it didn't come back to bite me in the ass.

After shit was squared away with Randi, we headed on down to Miami to finish off the summer right. Shit was awesome. All we did was enjoy shit. I had been smiling since the moment our plane left DC. The vacation was much needed. We had one week left in our month long vacation, when I got the phone call that broke my high spirits.

****

" *This Is For My Homies, See You When I Get There*"

Keeli, Juan and Asha are laying in the custom made king sized bed in the master suite asleep. The landline phone starts to ring. Keeli rolls over and answers it with her eyes still closed.

"Hello." Keeli says groggily.
"Baby, are you sleep?" Dana asks on the verge of tears.
"Nah. I'm up." Keeli half lies while rubbing her eyes. "What time is it?"
"It's 6:35 baby." Dana takes a deep breath. "Keeli, get up. Y'all gotta come home now."
"What? What are you talking about Ma?"
"Look, just come on home. I can't tell you over the phone."
Keeli sits up in the bed. "Come on Ma, it's too early for this. What's wrong?"
Dana starts to weep "They found Tiff and CoCo dead this morning Keeli. Jackie too."
Keeli jumps out the bed in shock "Ma please tell me you playing."
"No baby. They gone. All 3 of them. They never had a chance."
"Ma nooooooo" Keeli falls to her knees and begins to wail. Juan is startled awake. He jumps out the bed, just as Keeli rises to her feet and takes off out the bedroom. He runs behind her into the bathroom just as she starts to throw up in the toilet.
"What the hell is wrong with you?" Juan asks in a worried tone.
Keeli sits back on the floor and leans against the tub. She pulls her knees to her chest and continues to cry. "They gone Juan. They all gone."
"Who baby?" Juan asks as he kneels down beside Keeli and wipes her face and tries to comfort her.
"Tiffany, CoCo and Jackie." My sister and my cousin is gone. How am I supposed to tell CiCi his father dead? He just got him back and now he's gone." Keeli breaks down in Juan's arms. Juan looks up and sees CiCi standing in the doorway with tears in his eyes. Keeli looks up and sees CiCi and is unable to find the words she needs to comfort him.

"Looking up at CiCi, and seeing the tears he shed hurt so bad. I didn't know what to say to comfort my child. It was so much easier to explain to him that his father was gone to jail forever way back when. But this was different. Jackie had only been in CiCi's life a short time, but that time made a serious impression. Their bond was strong. It was like Jackie had never left. Now he was gone forever.

Juan went to CiCi and hugged him. I finally made it to my feel and joined them in a family embrace. I couldn't wrap my mind around the fact that I had lost my sister, my cousin and my first dude all in the same breath. Shit was not supposed to be like this. CoCo and Tiff were supposed to get their shit together and while we could have never done business together again, we was supposed to get back to rocking like family. And Jackie was supposed to be my right hand in continuing to raise our son. And now they were all gone. I couldn't get back to DC fast enough because I needed answers. I needed specifics and I was almost certain, I was gonna have to catch a few more bodies PERSONALLY because it was no way in hell you could kill my family and I not be the one to take you out your misery. We gathered the kids and got our stuff together and by 10:30 that morning, wheels were off the ground. By 1pm, we were landing in Leesburg. Juan took our kids and went home while me, CiCi and Adovia went straight to Dana's house where our family was assembling.

My aunt Maxine which was CoCo's mother was feeling the burn. She had treated her like shit when CoCo needed her the most. They spent YEARS not speaking and now CoCo was gone. I couldn't judge her though because my last encounter with both my sister and my cousin had been ugly. They needed my help and instead of helping them I turned my back on them. That shit was tearing my heart apart. My guilt was killing me as I sat among my family, I finally excused myself to go and call my father. I called and found out him and my grandma were already on their way to DC to claim Tiff's body. I called his cell and got no answer and I figured it was because he was driving and I knew my dad didn't like to talk while driving...and in this situation I wouldn't want him too. I left him a message letting him know I was home and to call me the minute they got in town.

Me and CiCi left Dana's and went to Jillian's. Jackie was her last son and while nobody ever said it, he had also been her favorite. Losing him, was like losing everything she needed to live. Yes she still had her daughter and her grandkids, but that would never fill l the void losing Jackie left in her heart. I felt so bad for her. She had a house full of people coming to pay their respects and she wouldn't stop cleaning. When everyone finally left, me CiCi, Jillian and her daughter Kemoni and her granddaughter rode out to Jackie's house in Forestville. His live in girlfriend Tarissa was there with her mother and sister. Now what I couldn't understand was why she seemed to be upset that I came with Jillian and CiCi. The whole time her and Jackie had been rocking, me and her had no issues. I knew her position and respected it and vice versa. But this day was different. I don't know if it was the hurt of losing Jackie that had her tripping or what, but she was throwing maddddd shade. Wasn't no point in being mad at me. Jackie was dead and gone, He couldn't do shit for either of us, my son or the baby she was four months pregnant with. It was no secret that Jill didn't like her ass, and even though I had moved on from her son, married someone else and had a whole starting lineup of babies, she still held me as her daughter in law and told me more than once that one day me and Jackie would get back together. But Tarissa couldn't be mad at me for how that woman felt. I never asked her to feel that way. CiCi got most of his stuff because he had to come back home now. While me and him gathered his stuff, Jill cleaned out Jackie's safe. I mean COMPLETELY. Then we left. She didn't ask Tarissa to participate in making the arrangements or nothing. I wanted to say something because I knew how Jackie felt about her due to our talks and I knew he would be heated with Jill for cutting her out like that. But I didn't. At the end of the day, Tarissa wasn't Jackie's wife…. Jill was his mother and I was just his ex, so it wasn't my place. We dropped them off and headed home.

While I had lost people near and dear to my heart on more than once occasion, I had never lost a parent so I truly didn't know how to even begin to approach this situation with my child. I tried to comfort him but he told me he just wanted some time alone for the moment. I had no choice but to respect his feelings and give him his space. The next morning, I went with CiCi, Jill and Kemoni to make the funeral arrangements. Jill called me before the sun came up and asked me to come. I didn't want to because it didn't feel like I should be a part of that, but I couldn't find the heart to tell her no. So I went. Once everything was said and done CiCi stayed with his Grandma and aunt. He said he wanted to help them get through this. I looked at my son and felt a mixture of pride and sadness. I was proud of the man he was becoming but I was sad that the weight of holding his grandmother together and burying his father was put on his shoulder. Since my dad and grandmother were in town, I went to the hotel to check on them. My father never called me, but my grandmother did so I knew when they arrived and where they were staying. I was feeling a little slighted that they didn't come to my house but I guess they figured not only did I lost my sister, but my cousin AND my baby father so I needed space. I always thought the loss of a relative is supposed to help bring a family closer. My meeting with my father that day showed me the exact opposite"

Keeli knocks on the door of room 451. Her grandmother Wanda opens the door. They share a hug and Wanda kisses Keeli on the cheek.

"How you holding up baby?" Wanda asks.
"I'm about as alright as I'mma be right now grandma."
"I know baby. Trust me I know." Wanda closes and locks the door.
Keeli goes and sits in the chair, while Wanda sits on one of the beds.
"Where's my daddy?"
"He in the bathroom baby. He should be out soon."
"Just y'all two came?"
"Yeah. Her mama couldn't take it."
"Grandma, I feel so bad. Like most of this is my fault."
"And you should!" Alvin's voice booms as he walks out of the bathroom with tears rolling down his face.
"Alvin listen…" Wanda tries to defuse the confrontation.
"No Mama! I gotta get this off my chest! I done been quiet too long and now I gotta put my child in the ground!" Alvin wipes his eyes as he tries to regain his composure to no avail. "You got her up here and involved in all this stupid shit you out here doing! You might as well had pulled the trigger your goddamn self!"
"Hold up!" Keeli jumps up off the bed. "Now Daddy, I told you myself a while back that me and Tiffany didn't even talk anymore. Now Tiff was grown just like me! She made her own decisions! I'm just as fucked up as everybody else that she gone but you aint about to stand here and pin this shit on me! No fucking way!"
Alvin chuckles and shakes his head in disbelief. "You know, I never thought I would see the day when I hated a child of mine… But you Keeli…. Only God could understand the hatred I feel for you. And I swear on a stack of bibles that stretch 10 miles high that I wish it was your ass we were burying instead of Tiffany."
"Alvin!" Wanda yells as she stands in front of him. "Now I'm not gonna sit here and let you talk to that girl like that! Life and death are God's will NOT MAN."

"It's the truth mama!" Alvin begins to cry again as he points an angry finger in Keeli's face. "Tiffany had a future ahead of her before she got mixed up with you! But I guess since you fucked up your own life, you had to go and fuck up hers too! You aint good for shit but what you doing now! Selling drugs and popping out fucking babies! You are a fucking carbon copy of your no good ass mother!"

"Now that's enough! Alvin I swear…" Wanda attempts to go in on her son but Keeli interrupts her.

"It's okay grandma. He's just speaking what's in his heart." Keeli takes a deep breath in an attempt to keep control of her own emotions. "Look, I'm not gonna be at the funeral, but I would like to pay for the services."

"No! Hell NO!" Alvin yells. "You keep your money! We don't want no parts of that filthy shit. I'll tell you what to do with it. Put it in a fund to pay for the services of yourself or your kids. Because you too fucking stupid to see that this shit aint gonna end here!! Soon and real soon, Dana gonna find herself dropping your ass in the ground. And as long as I live, I will pray that you die a slow and painful death just like my child did and that your nothing ass burns in hell for all eternity." Alvin turns and walks back into the bathroom and slams the door.

"Baby…" Wanda begins to try and comfort Keeli.

"It's okay Grandma." Keeli forces a smile to her face. "I'm okay. I'ma go ahead and leave. Give my condolences to the rest of the family."

"Keeli listen…." Wanda calls out for her with her own tears starting to fall. Keeli walks out the door, never bothering to look back.

"I forced myself to be so strong at this point, it even scared me. I fought back those tears from the elevator, to the lobby and all the way down to my car. I didn't want anybody to see me cry. But once I was alone in my car, behind the privacy of those tents, I let go. I couldn't hold it any longer. Every word my father spoke replayed in my mind and cut so deep into my heart. I kept wondering if I was really that bad of a person. I mean to have one's own father wish not just death but a slow and painful death upon them.

What do you think?

Really, I don't give a fuck with nobody thinks. I KNOW I'm not that fucked up and didn't deserve all that shit he just threw at me. I tried to be there for Tiffany, but what nobody seemed to understand was this wasn't the same 15 year old who ran away on a Greyhound bus to come stay with me. I took care of that little girl. I made sure she graduated high school and all that shit. But this here was a grown ass woman. A woman who had gone through shit, a woman who chose her own paths in life. I never wanted my life for ANY of my siblings but as ADULTS I couldn't force them out of the streets. Tiff chose to live her life the way she did so how the fuck could he really blame me.

Why didn't his bitch ass blame himself for BOTH OF US? Nah, he was too bitch to swallow that pill.

Maybe if he was a better father, provided a better life for me instead of leaving him when I needed him the most… maybe I wouldn't have gotten mixed up in this shit at all. Then Tiff wouldn't have tried to follow suit. Fuck him and fuck anybody else who felt I was the blame for this shit. And what's crazy is he talking all this shit about keep all my filthy money, yeah he would bark that shit now. Last time I checked, that big ass house he got and all three of them Cadillacs his bitch ass drove… the CTS, the STS AND the Escalade XLT…. I paid for all that shit. Me and my filthy money. The money to start his home improvement business and his wife daycare, I GAVE them that shit. Not loaned but GAVE THEM. Who the fuck had been paying for my brother to attended fucking Berkley since last August? Not the bank, Not the United Negro College Fund and damn sure not his bitch ass. It was ME. Everything I did for them and everybody else I did simply because I wanted us all to be living our dreams no matter what they were. I was wealthy beyond my wildest imagination. Why not share it with my family. I was worth more than Michael Jackson, Bill Gates AND Master P. I made more a year than the fucking President of the United States. His salary was play money compared to what I was bringing home. And when I die, I couldn't take a dime of it with me. So why not share the wealth?

I knew niggas all across the United States making MAJOR figures. They riding around in Bentley's and Double R's but their people… they got their people living completely FUCKED UP. I'm talking about project slumming, collecting state aid and stamps. What kinda shit was that? If I fucked with you and you living grimey, it's simply because you chose to. Wasn't no two ways about it. So fuck Alvin and anybody else who had something negative to say about me.

I got my cry on and then said fucked that nigga and went on home to the people I knew loved me without a doubt. Over the next week, I helped Jill get everything together for Jackie's funeral. Me and CiCi wrote his obituary together. On that following Monday, we laid CoCo to rest. Her service was packed. She had done a lot of people wrong in her last days, but she was still my blood so I know a lot of the motherfuckas showed their face out of respect for me. It was hard as shit to sit there and know that white casket surrounded by some of the most beautiful flowers I had ever seen held my girl inside of it. Maxine opted for a closed casket because the drugs had ate her body up so bad and part of her face was literally GONE from where she had been shot at. I felt so bad for my aunt Max. Her guilt was killing her and she could barely breathe. When they lowered CoCo into the ground my heart ached. My nigga was truly gone. I would have given anything to be able to go back to the last time I laid eyes on my family. I would've still whooped both their asses but instead of leaving them to die, I would've drug them by their hair to the nearest inpatient treatment facility and got them some help. Nobody actually said it, but we all knew somehow, some way their newfound habit played a part in this shit. What I didn't understand was how Jackie ended up mixed up in this shit because he had supposedly cut ties with Tiff. So nothing made sense.

As we headed back to the cars, Me and Ciaira were shoulder to shoulder crying when I spotted a face in the crowd I hadn't expected to ever see again. Monae. I felt like I was looking at a ghost. She looked almost scared when we made eye contact. But losing my cousin and sister... having just walked away from the hole in the ground that would forever hold the shell of my nigga, I was ready to forgive all those who had trespassed against me. Life was short. Too short and at any given time your number could come up. It was time to make some serious life changes. Without another word, I left Ciaira side and walked over to Monae and embraced her. We hugged each other and just cried. Ciaira came over and joined the hug and the three of us just cried and cried. When we left the cemetery we all went to the repass where we partied for CoCo. It was all love all around the club it was held in. People spoke about the CoCo they used to know. The fun loving, tell it like it is, ride with you the end CoCo. Nobody wanted to talk about the turmoil she spent her last days in. At the repass we played catch up with Monae. She told us she had graduated from the UMES and was now teaching at an elementary school in St. Mary's county. Her and her kid's father had got back together and were happily married. I was proud of her. She was happy and we were happy for her. We forgave each other for all that went down between us and exchanged numbers. We all knew shit would never be like it was, but we were all willing to work together to rebuild our friendship, our sisterhood, like we had back in the days we were kicking in her 2 bedroom section 8 joint around Azzee Bates.

On Tuesday, Jackie was laid to rest. My family attended minus the obvious... my husband. Jill fainted and Tarissa had to be removed three separate times. At the repass, something dawned on me. Simm was NOT there. I knew they had their fallout back before Jackie passed but that was his A1. That shit wasn't supposed to matter no more. Then it registered that he hadn't been at CoCo's service either and she was supposed to have been his woman. I instantly didn't feel right about none of this. I had a heart full of suspicion, but I kept them to myself and continued to celebrate the life and legacy of the first man I ever loved. It all was getting to be too much for me, so I went outside to get some air. That's where I bumped into Tarissa alone and lent her a shoulder to cry on. While we were talking I asked her had she heard from Simm. And she told me a story that confirmed my suspicions. She said the night Jackie was killed, he had been at home with her. They were working on the baby's nursery. Simm called him and Jackie told her he would be back. He had to go meet Simm in Northeast. So she couldn't understand how he ended up naked, bound, gagged and executed in a bed with two women out in Upper Marlboro. I knew then without a shadow of doubt Simm had done this. The only way I would believe different is if somebody had told me his ass was dead too and I had been the one to pull the trigger. When I got home that night, I hated to bother Maxine but I had questions so I called her. She said they initial police report said that the incident had been a robbery, but they had changed that because it was determined that the door had been broken from the inside and even more so the three body had been placed together after they were murdered to set the stage. They determined that when they found Tiffany's blood and bits of her skull in the basement.

So like I said I knew it was him….. Now I just needed to know WHY.

I waited two weeks after the funeral when the dust had settled and pulled a pop up around Todd Place hoping to catch Simm on the scene. I knew this nigga created the hole in my heart where my sister, cousin and baby father used to dwell and I was determined I was gonna put a couple slugs in his head. But to my surprise, he wasn't on the scene. I dropped my number with his man Roland and told him to make sure Simm got it. I had been Simm's weakness for longer than I cared to remember, so I knew he would jump out a 20 story window for the chance to rap to me. So now I just had to sit back and wait for his sneaky ass to come ringing my bell and then I would ring his. But for now all I could do was wait.

The next three months seemed to go by in the blink of an eye. Everything was calm. The streets and my life. I still hadn't heard from Simm but I knew he would pop up eventually. I wasn't sweating it though. I was just focusing on living. My marriage was in an amazing place. It's hard to explain the place those three months lead me and Juan to but we were inseparable. We loved harder and stronger than we ever had. Back in the days when shit was all fucked up between us, I would've never seen this place of peace and love between us. But I soon realized it was the real calm before the storm.

At three months away from giving birth to the last of our crew, something went terribly wrong. Some shit I never thought about in all the years I had known Juan. In all honesty, nothing in my life had every hurt this bad. Even now, years later, I still wake up sometimes in the middle of the night in cold sweats, shaking like a leaf and crying tears I couldn't stop even if I wanted to. I never knew a pain like this was humanly possible, but it was and I felt it.

To me, this was far worse than being shot, stabbed, beaten or strangled. This was the type of pain that made you beg God to just take you. You found yourself praying for death and it just wouldn't come. You have no choice but to suffer through it. But like they say, what don't kill you only serves to make you stronger.

****

" Like You'll Never See Me Again"

Juan is laying in the bed watching the 10 O'clock news while Keeli is beside him eating a bowl of ice cream. "I was thinking of smoking the turkey for Thanksgiving." Keeli says between shoveling scoops of ice cream in her mouth."

"That baby got you greedy as shit." Juan chuckles. "You shoveling ice cream while thinking about smoked turkeys."

"Shut up." Keeli laughs and playfully hits him in the arm. "You know this my season and I like to have shit in order."

"I know baby. I'm just messing with you." Juan leans over and kisses her lips softly and lovingly.

"And before I forget, next Friday, we gotta stay in the hotel. The people coming to do the carpets and the floors."

"How much they charging you?"

"3200."

"We could've did that shit ourselves."

"Nigga please. I'm six months pregnant. What I look like cleaning carpets?" Keeli slurps the ice cream off her spoon.

"Is it really that good?" Juan asks while looking at Keeli with a mixture of lust and love in his eyes.

"Yep." Keeli smiles and slurps again.

"You over there slurping and shit. I got something you can slurp on."

"You so damn nasty." Keeli blushes.

"I'm serious Mami." Juan snuggles up to Keeli and starts to rub on her thighs. "You been bullshitting all week."

"No. You might hurt the baby." Keeli giggles.

Juan chuckles. "Stop playing and come on Keeli before I get mad." Juan playfully bites Keeli's breast through her nightgown.

"Papi knew my spot and once he started nibbling tiddies, nightgown and all it was on. It had been a long week and I

know I had been slacking on my wifely duties. Not because of lack of interest or desire to be with my husband, but due to pure exhaustion for us both. By time we would make it to bed at night, we would be sleep before our heads hit the pillows. The only reason we were up this late tonight is because we had managed to get a nap in earlier. And I was so glad we did because we both NEEDED each other that night.

After we finished it was a little after 11. We both were officially spent. We laid there for a few minutes debating who was gonna go get the wash cloth. I felt like it should've been him because well, I was pregnant and I rode that nigga until my legs cramped up on my ass…and still kept going because he was cumming and I respected his nut. While we were both were pleading our cases on who should go get the washcloths and why, sleep crept into our room. We both were butt naked, sleeping like babies until CiCi came and woke us up a little after 1am."

CiCi knocks on the door to the master suite then opens it. He walks in the room and to the bed and slightly shakes Juan until he begins to stir. "Pops, Randi on the phone."
"Huh?" Juan asks while stretching and still half asleep."
"Randi on the phone."
"Tell her I'm sleep man."
"Nah pops. She crying and wanted to know if I had talked to Ti today."
"Alright." Juan sits up and grabs the cordless phone on the nightstand. CiCi turns and leaves the room. Keeli sits up and listens to Juan's once sided conversation with Randi on the phone. "Hello… Listen, calm down…Did you call her cell? Alright, I'm on my way right now." Juan hangs up the phone and gets out the bed.
"What's going on Papi?"
"She saying Ti aint come home from school today."
"Are you serious? Did she call her cell?" Keeli asks in concern.

"Yeah. It's going straight to voicemail."

"She probably hanging out with her little girlfriends."

"Man its damn near 2 in the morning. I aint tryna hear that shit. The minute she walk through that door, I'ma fix all this." Juan replies as he walks into the bathroom and finally washes off him and Keeli's love making. When he's done, he walks back into the bedroom and begins to get dressed.

"You want me to come with you?" Keeli asks sweetly.

"Nah, you and my little man get some rest. I wont be long." Juan grabs his cell phone and walks over to Keeli. He kisses her softly on the lips and then kisses her belly. "I love you Mami." Juan says genuinely as he smiles at her.

"I love you too Papi." Keeli blushes. "Drive safely baby."

"I will. Turn the ringer back on cause I'ma call you."

"Okay." Keeli replies as Juan leaves out the room.

"I hated to say it, but I knew it wouldn't be long before she started smelling herself. TiTi was 16, cute, fly and had was starting to get a little body on her. I told Juan I didn't think it was a good idea to let her transfer to school in DC, but noooooo. His little princess wanted to change schools. So she was practically living with Randi now and came here on the weekends….sometimes. I just kept thinking how if her ass was here with us, right now she would be down the hall sleep…. Instead her hot ass was more than likely somewhere with her legs in the air. Like Dana used to always say, Aint shit open after midnight but the emergency room and legs. And with Ti's newfound attitude I was willing to bed it was legs.

I finally got up and went into the bathroom to clean myself up. Once I was done, I found myself hungry again. So I put my nightgown back on, grabbed my comforter and pillow and headed downstairs. I knew I wasn't gonna be able to sleep until Juan got back so I set up camp in the family room. I went in the kitchen and hooked me up a big ass cold chicken sandwich, grabbed some doritos and an apple juice. Then I got comfortable on the sectional and watched TV while I ate. Before I knew it, I was out again. Sleeping hard until about 4:30 am when Papi came in the house with Randi in tow."

Keeli jumps up from her sleep when she hears the front door close and the chime beep. "Papi is that you?" She calls out from the family room. "Yeah man, go back to sleep." Juan says as he continues down the hall and goes down into the basement. Keeli gets up and walks out of the family room where she finds Randi sitting in one of the antique chairs in the foyer. Her eyes are bloodshot red and puffy as a continuous stream of tears continue to fall down her face.
"What's going on? Did y'all find Ti?"
"He's here Keeli." Maranda says in a shaky voice, trying to speak through her tears. "He's here and he has my baby." Randi sobs hard
"What?" Keeli asks confused. "Who? What are you talking about?"
"Armend. I tried to tell you before that was not Aleksander you met. Aleksander is dead. Armend is his twin. He killed him. Now he is here Keeli. He kidnapped my baby and they want 25 million dollars and the password by 5am or they gonna kill her." Randi sobs uncontrollably at the thought. "I just want my baby back." Keeli walks over and hugs Randi as silent tears begin to fall from her eyes. "I'm so scared Keeli. They have my baby. She doesn't deserve this."
"Just calm down Randi. Ti is gonna be safe in your arms before you know it."
"I pray so Keeli. You don't know the evil of this man. He killed his own brother, his twin, in cold blood over some fucking money. He killed his nephew, my son and didn't blink. Ti means nothing to him. He can have all the money, I just want my daughter back."
"Stay right here. I'm gonna go check on Juan." Keeli goes down the hall and walks down into the basement. She walks through the laundry room and into the "vault". Juan is grabbing money off the shelf and putting it into duffle bags. "Papi..." Keeli calls out nervously to him.
Juan turns around and he has tears rolling down his face. Keeli walks over to him and hugs him. "I swear Keeli, if one hair on her head is out of place..."

"Papi don't think like that. She is gonna be okay."

"She better. For Randi sakes. Cause if they hurt my baby, I swear I'ma kill that bitch. I should've known she was in some shit when she came running back here after all this time."

"Don't worry about that right now. Let's just focus on getting TiTi back home safe."

"You right baby."

"Anything you need me to do?" Keeli asks sincerely.

"Yeah. I want you to go upstairs with the kids. Make sure they safe. And when I leave, lock the doors and make sure the alarm is set. Don't move or touch a phone until I walk back in this house."

"Okay." Keeli kisses Juan softly on the lips. She turns to walk away and he pulls her back to him and hugs her tight. He looks in her eyes and smiles. "Keeli, I love you girl."

"I love you too baby. With all my heart."

"And I'm sorry for anything I ever did to hurt you." Juan says sincerely.

"That's all in the past. I let it go and now it's time for you to do the same. I love you Juan and I know you love me. Nothing in the world could ever change that."

"You right." Juan kisses Keeli's lips softly and no more words are spoken as she leaves the vault. Juan turns around and continues to put the money into the bags.

"When I walked out of that room I felt so bad for both Juan and Randi. I couldn't imagine the pain of knowing your child's fate was resting in someone else hands. I had never seen Juan cry before, and looking at him that morning broke my heart. He loved all his children including CiCi and I guess even thinking about what Ti may be experiencing was too much to handle. I did know one thing for sure, the minute she was home safe, motherfuckas was gonna start dying because this was shit I knew Juan was not going for under any circumstances. Sure he would pay that ransom to ensure her safe return but I knew my husband well enough to know he would leave no stone unturned when it came to

finding these niggas and touching any and everybody they ever said hello to. As I walked up the stairs I decided then that once Ti was home safely, I would tell my husband about my meeting with this sick motherfucka while I was in Milan. Would he be mad with me? Of course. But the last thing I wanted was for him to get that bit of information from anywhere else in the world and have it looking like I had some shit to hide. I decided then I wasn't even gonna wait. I busted a U turn and headed back downstairs and into the vault. I told him I needed to talk to him right now and he told me whatever it was had to wait because he was on a timer. I understood and decided not to press because I didn't want him to be a millisecond late for the drop. I turned and went back upstairs to the sleeping quarters where our children were.

I woke up CiCi and had him help me bring the twins and Asha into me and Juan's room. The four of them got comfortable in the bed and I chilled on the chaise. I was wide awake with a mind and heart full of worry so no sleep was coming my way. I closed my eyes and said a silent prayer for Ti's safety. I prayed it all would be over soon and we could get back to living.

When I opened my eyes, I found myself focusing on our wedding picture that hung on the wall in the sitting area of our master suite. I just stared at it and thought back to that day. I smiled as I thought of the joy and love Juan brought to my life from the very beginning. He was my rock and I was his. We needed each other to survive in this world. I couldn't wait until we were old and gray, sitting out in the backyard with our grandchildren, stealing kisses from each other when nobody was looking.

I heard the front door chime again signaling it was opened. Not even a minute later, I heard Juan's truck doors close. Suddenly, I felt different. I felt anxious and nervous. My palms were sweating and my throat was so dry. My left eye started jumping like crazy. Ever since I was little, I believed the saying that when your left eye jumped, something bad was about to happen. My shit felt like it was about to jump out of the socket at that moment.

I shot up off the chaise and my legs started moving. I passed my sleeping children, peacefully sleeping in our bed without a care in the world. I felt like I was being moved by an unseen force. I didn't know where I was going but I had to get there urgently. I could hear my heart thumping in my chest as it raced what felt like a mile a minute. I got halfway down the spiral stairs and that's when it happened.

The moment that changed my life forever.

As I ran down the stairs, I got a sharp pain in my heart that stopped me dead in my tracks. The next sound I heard was what I know to be unmistakable sound of the Russian assault rifle known as the AK47. It wasn't just one, I could tell because it sounded like the Fourth Of July outside. It was the longest 60 seconds of my life. I was frozen in space. All I could do was stand in shock and listen.

When the shots ended, I heard multiple cars screeching away. My body felt so cold. Tears started to roll without warning or invitation. I headed for the door in nothing but my nightgown. No shoes, no coat, hell I didn't even have panties on. When I got outside, everything around me was a blur. I couldn't see anything. I couldn't even think. My feet continued to move along the cold, wet asphalt of my driveway. The closer I got to the end of the driveway, the more tears fell. When I finally made it to the end, my entire body went numb. I couldn't feel anything. And til this very day I still believe that pain in my chest as I came down the stairs was my heart breaking because it knew what I would find when I got outside and it couldn't take that pain."

Juan is laying on the ground beside the driver side of his Range Rover in a puddle of his own blood. His eyes are wide open and focused straight above at the night sky. His body is covered with blood. There are more than 200 bullet holes in his Range Rover. The driver's side back door is wide open and the duffle bags of money are gone. On the inside of the truck, Randi's lifeless bullet riddle body is laying across the passenger seat. The inside of the truck is covered with blood. Keeli kneels down on the ground beside Juan. She lifts his lifeless torso and cradles him in her arms and begins to rock back and forth as unstoppable tears continue to roll down her face.

"It hurt like hell to only be able to hold the shell of what was the love of my life. Juan was my heart, my rock, my everything. And in the blink of an eye, he was gone just like that. No notice, no warning, no chance to say goodbye.

I wanted to scream but couldn't find my voice. It felt like I didn't have an ounce of breath left in my body. There was nothing but pain. An indescribable pain. CiCi came out and tried to get me to come back in the house, but I couldn't. I couldn't feel my son touching me or hear him talking to me. I wanted to just lay down and die. When the police arrived, they had to pry Juan out of my arms. CiCi sat on the cold curb with me and held me as I continued to cry. I still hadn't lost it yet. That didn't come until the coroner arrived and they zipped Juan up in that bag. That's when I realized that as much as I wanted this shit to be a dream, it wasn't. My husband had really been murdered. He was really gone from life. I was really alone. THAT'S when I lost it. I stared screaming and tried to fight the police when they grabbed me up as I made my way towards the coroner at full speed. I refused to let him go. I know they wanted to taze my ass out there but I guess they also knew I was truly in pain having lost my husband…right at the foot of our castle. It took a while but they finally got me back up the driveway and into my house. That's when they police started trying to interview me but I couldn't stop crying long enough to say anything. All I could think about was Juan and the fact that he was dead.

By 7am, the house was filled with family and friends and everybody was hurting. Nobody could believe Juan was really gone. My pajamas were covered with his blood but I wouldn't take them off. I was in a state of shock. CiCi had talked to the police for me when it was just us and he told them about Ti being missing. A little after 9:30, they came baring more bad news. They believed they had found her and needed someone to come identify her body. The body they found had been recovered from a ditch about 300 yards from where Juan and Randi were murdered at. They came upon the body as they were searching the area. By noon it was confirmed that it was indeed my step daughter they found in the ditch. She had been raped, beaten, burned repeatedly with cigarettes, strangled and finally shot in the back of the head twice.

For the next two days, I couldn't eat or sleep. All I could do was cry. Dana didn't want me staying in that house anymore, but I refused to leave. She took the kids and CiCi, Syrus and Ciaira stayed with me. 3 days later Ian and his family arrived. They stayed at my house also. The day after they got there, we had a huge dilemma to deal with. Ian wanted his son buried in Colombia at his family's cemetery on his property. He had already contacted Randi's family and made the arrangements to have her body shipped to them in Guatemala. He was footing the whole bill for them. Then there was Sissy. She wanted Juan and Ti both buried in Jamaica. It was said that she was planning to leave and go back to Jamaica because she couldn't take being in the same place she lost her son at. When we all got together at Sissy's house for dinner, shit got real ugly real fast. Ian and Sissy started arguing. They both blamed each other for Juan's death. I got up and just walked out without a word. I couldn't take it. My husband was dead and gone. He left me behind to raise four kids AND the baby I was carrying ALONE. To stand there and listen to them argue over him like he was a damn shirt or something... It was either leave or go off the deep end. So I chose to leave. Me and Ian had always had a great relationship and I wanted to keep it that way. I left, but before I did, with a face full of tears I let them know they could argue until they both lost their voices. They could go on and fight and kill each other for all I cared. None of that shit mattered to me. BUT I needed them to know, understand and most importantly RESPECT that my husband was being buried right here in the United States point blank.

When Ian got back to the house that night, once everyone else was asleep me and him sat up and talked. When we went to bed that night, Ian was standing in my corner, understanding that although Juan was his son, he was my husband and we had a life together right here that included our kids. When Sissy got the news the next day she was livid. I really didn't care anymore. The little bit of composure I held all those years that kept me off her ass was out of respect for my husband. My husband was now gone, so I had already made it up in my mind I was done playing with this bitch. If she ever spoke to me sideways again I was gonna tear that bitch head slam off her shoulders using nothing but my bare hands…. Yeah, my disdain for this bitch was that serious.

I realized when we stepped out the door heading to begin the pain process of making funeral arrangements for my love and my step daughter I had a huge support system. It was no way I would have made it through that day without my father in law, two of my sister in laws, my brother in law and Juan's best friend/ cousin Roc. I cried the entire day because with every final decision that was made, it was becoming more and more real to me. Since that day back in Panama when "Mr. Bundy" walked out into that courtyard I KNEW Juan was my forever love. I always thought me and him would grow old and gray together. I always thought our children would have to bury us together because one of us would die from old age when we were like damn near 100 and the next day the other would die from a broken heart because we couldn't take being a part from each other. Yeah I know, it sounds farfetched as hell but who really thinks about living life alone because the man who you feel like you were born specifically from his rib FOR HIM was gone? I never thought I would be left all alone.

But here I was.

The week leading up to the funeral was pure hell for me. I had to write his obituary with Tia and it was so painful reliving his life through words. Then picking out his clothes was unbearable. Thanksgiving was that Thursday, Ciaira who had been by my side since the day Juan was killed finally took a break. Her and the kids went down south that Wednesday and were coming home Saturday. CiCi and Sy went to my mother's house where my family was having dinner ar. Ian and his clan went to Tia's. I turned down all invitations because I just wanted to be alone. I stayed in my bed and cried all day. This was the first time I had been home alone since Juan passed and yes I started freaking out. I kept expecting him to walk through that door at any moment. But that moment never came. He was really and truly gone.

On Saturday, my kids finally came home and I was left to deal with the overwhelming and painful task of explaining to my babies that their daddy and big sister would never come home again. They were now in heaven.

This was a pain I wouldn't wish on my worst enemy.

Monday morning rolled around and it was time for us to stand as a family and say goodbye to my love of a lifetime. The night before was the first night I actually slept more than two or three hours since Juan was murdered. I believe it was because of the dream I had. I dreamt that he was lying right next to me in our bed. He was holding me close like he always did. I could literally smell him in my dream. He told me not to worry because him and Ti were alright. They were at peace and would always be with us. He told me that he needed me to be strong and hold it down for our kids, because if I fell apart, they would too. He told me he needed me to survive. He kissed me and told me even death couldn't stop him from loving me as much as he did every single day that he was alive. He kissed me one last time and then I woke up. It was 7am. The sun was extremely bright for 7am in November. I smiled, still feeling the effects of my husband presences... then I looked over to my right and saw that his side of the bed was still empty, as it had been since the morning he got that phone call. I couldn't hold it in as I cried like a baby. I held his pillow and didn't even try to fight the pain that was trying to escape my heart.

This couldn't be life.

We walked into that funeral home and had it not been for my son and my brother holding me up I know I would have passed out. The walk down that aisle was the longest walk ever for me. When we finally got to the front where him and Ti were side by side, my heart couldn't take it. He was really gone. I was really alone.

During the combined services, there wasn't a dry eye in the place. My baby would definitely be missed and so would Ti. After the funeral, we all went to the cemetery. Juan's homeboy LaLa and his wife sang a duet of It's So Hard To Say Goodbye as both caskets, Juan's in black and Ti's in snow white were lowered into the ground. Simultaneously, two white doves were released into the air to represent their souls finally being free. When the pastor said his final prayer, everyone released a white balloon into the air honoring Juan and Infiniti's memory.

The repass followed right after the cemetery visit. We had it at a huge hall out in Rockville because it was way too many people who wanted to share in the Homegoing celebration for two people who were gone far too soon. By time we finally got home that night, I was exhausted. The whole day had been both mentally and physically draining. Me and all four of my kids climbed into me and Juan's bed because none of us wanted to be alone. Losing him and Ti the way we did was a reminder that life is not promised. As my babies slept, I laid awake and said a prayer for each of them that God would protect them. They were all I had left in this world. All the money and material things I risked life and limb for all of those years now meant absolutely nothing. I thanked God for protecting us all these years and made a promise to myself and God to get this street shit out of my life ASAP. It was time. I also asked God to give me the strength I needed to keep living every day without my AIR. I asked for the strength I needed to be the mother those four people lying beside me needed me to be. I asked for peace, said amen and then closed my eyes.

It felt like I had been sleep for 10 minutes but it had been hours. And while I slept, my conscious decided to remind me of something. That same dream I had when I was in Milan came back to revisit me. Only this time I could see things so much more clearly. It wasn't the devil standing there laughing while Randi pleaded with me and I stood there like a fool with blood on my hands….. It was the motherfucka I THOUGHT was Maranda's husband Aleksander…. His twin brother Armend. It all made sense now. Without even realizing it, I signed my husband and step daughter death certificate. In my dream, I turned to look behind me with those same bloody hands and saw Juan and Ti both laying in the same caskets that I picked out for them. The same caskets I stood with a broken heart and watch be lowered into the ground just hours before. Armend then looked at me and said "We couldn't have done it without you." and broke out into this crazed laughter like the fucking lunatic he was. I woke up screaming, sweating and crying.

It all made sense now.

That dream had been a warning, but I took it for what I wanted it to be and now my family had a huge hole in it where Juan and Ti once sat. CiCi tried to comfort me, but that realization left me inconsolable. There was nothing I could do to erase or change what I had done and I was gonna have to live with that pain forever."

****

"What's Done In The Dark"

"The next two weeks, I can't even tell you how I made it through because I truly don't know. My heart was so heavy I couldn't eat or sleep. I didn't leave the house, all I did was cry. The realization of what I had done had me secretly contemplating suicide. The only other person who knew about my meeting with Armend while I was in Milan was Ciaira, so I confided my guilt in her. I also confided my fear. Because the moment Juan and Ti were put in the ground, Ian and his family got on their shit looking for whoever thought they were gonna touch his family and live to celebrate it. Ian's reach was GLOBAL and from my understanding he was leaving no stone unturned in trying to find out the who, what, and why of his son and granddaughter's murder. Everybody had been saying they knew it had something to do with Maranda. Just nobody knew WHAT except me and Ciaira. I was praying it stayed that way because while my heart usually pumped no fear, I knew Ian was capable of becoming a fucking terrorist when need be. I had heard far too many stories about the way this man moved. My team was strong, but not that strong...

On this day, I was forced to leave my house because it was the day of the reading of Juan's will. We all had to meet at his attorney's office in Downtown DC. I didn't want to be there, but I had to because I was his wife. And once again it was proven that everything happens for a reason. At first I was gonna stay home and just come another time and sign whatever I needed to sign and be done with it. I really didn't feel comfortable being around people. At times, I wondered if they could look at me and see what I had done. Ciaira insisted I go. Her reasoning was Sissy is shiesty as shit, and without me sitting right there, who knows what type of strings she may pull to fuck around and get my kids cut out his will. At first I was like so what, they will be fine but like she said this aint about me. This is about them and Juan would be PISSED if I didn't go. She was right, so I got myself together and drove. I don't know why I decided to drive but boy was I glad I did.

We all sat in the conference room. I thought we were just getting papers to look over and sign but that wasn't the case. Juan had done a videotaped last will and testament so we had to watch it and then there would be a paper signing session. They were all talking about going to lunch afterwards. I didn't know about all that, although I was showing face I felt like I betrayed my husband, my family and myself. I really just wanted to handle this and then go crawl back in my bed and cry. His attorney started the video and everybody smiled as Juan appeared on the screen. I couldn't help but begin to cry silent tears. I peeped Sissy roll her eyes at me, but I didn't blame her. The reason we were sitting there was my fault.

Juan greeted us with his usual charm and humor then he got serious. He said he hoped it was 100 years before we had to view this, but in the event that it wasn't, he wanted us each to know he loved us and while he knew the things he was leaving us with wouldn't replace him, he hoped we would take them in his memory and just be strong until we met again. I looked around as everybody was wiping tears.

In his will, he left his share of Bundy Enterprises in Colombia to Roc. That was the coke farm. He left his share of the Bundy Enterprises Real Estate Company to Mikey along with all the profits. He left 25 million dollars to be split equally between his nieces and nephews and God Children, so they each ended up with a little over 1.6 million dollars each. Each of his sisters got 5 million dollars. He left Sissy his ocean front property in Jamaica and three businesses that he owned there…. And I knew nothing about this property or these businesses. I felt a tad bit slighted but was like okay, aint nothing I can do about that. It's cool. Let's move on…. We all got secrets right. Cause God knows I walking around with a hum-fucking-dinger on my heart. He left Ian, who came back for this because it was what his son requested his love and gratitude and eternal thanks for the life he provided him while he was here on this earth. I always knew Juan loved his dad, but listening to the words he spoke to Ian from that tape…. It made even the strongest man in that room, my father in law cry. Juan even lost a few tears while he expressed his love and gratitude to his father. Like he said, Ian had everything in this world he could ever want and more…

To our three sons, he left them his G4, his yacht and home in Amsterdam…and this was more shit I had no clue about. He also left a 25 million dollar trust fund to be split between the 3 of them. They would each get their share when they turned 25. He left Infiniti and Asha his home, yacht and G4 that was located in Spain. By now I was like hold up….what the entire fuck is going on. Because again, this was more shit I knew nothing about. I didn't say anything because what difference would it have made. It wasn't like I could walk into our house or pick up the phone and ask him why he felt the need to hide so much from me. So I sat there and listened, although inside yeah, I was feeling some kind of way. I thought we were better than this. He also left Ti and

Asha a 25 million dollar trust fund with the same stipulations as our sons. Sissy shocked me when she asked the Attorney to stop the video briefly. She wanted to know if it was possible for his will to be changed. I just knew this was when I was about to flip out and kill this bitch with my bare hands but she surprised me. She wanted to know if it could be changed since Ti was deceased and have her inheritance transferred to the baby I was carrying once it was born and had a name. I think everybody in that room was shocked because well, me and Sissy were oil and water and since the shit that went down at her house that night when they had me arrested, I aint have no words for her and vice versa. Even when we had the dinner at her house after Juan died, me and her didn't say a word to each other. I only went because Ian insisted I come. The lawyer said he would draft up the necessary documents that week.

We went back to the video and I swear I wish it would have ended when Sissy interrupted. I wish the video would've broke and I was never able to hear the next words that came from Juan's mouth.

All that fucking time, right under my nose, Juan ass had been living a double life. Juan had a WHOLE NOTHER FAMILY….. with none other than that bitch THE FENDI QUEEN. They had two fucking kids together. A little boy who was 3. His name was… wait for it…

Juan Moreno Jr!

They also had a little girl. She was 1 years old. Turns out, she turned 1 on the day Juan was killed. Her name was Niesha. This motherfucka had been playing me the ENTIRE TIME. He left the kids the same trust fund as our kids, his home, yacht and jet in Australia, He even left the bitch

Niema 10 million dollars for herself.

It's no way this shit is for real was all I kept thinking. Next thing I knew the office was in a complete uproar. Everybody was yelling and shit because everybody knew that if nobody else knew about this bitch and her bastards Roc and Mikey asses knew and never said a mumbling fucking word. It took 20 minutes to get everybody to calm down so the attorney could go back to playing the tape. I sat there during the argument and said not a word. I periodically chuckled to myself because this shit was unbelievable. Juan started saying some shit about hoping I could find it in my heart to forgive him and blah blah fucking blah.

I got up with what little bit of dignity I had left from that low blow his coward ass waited until he was dead and gone to deliver. I grabbed my purse, bid everyone a good day and left.

FUCK JUAN.

I held my head until I got in my car. I punched that steering wheel so hard I thought I may have broken my hand at one point. I wanted to do nothing more than drive out to the cemetery and dig that motherfucker up and kill his ass again myself. He played the shit outta me and I couldn't get past that.

I couldn't wrap my mind around how stupid I had been. I actually believed his trifling, foul, lying ass was true to me. I didn't want shit from him and had decided my kids wasn't taking part in that bullshit either. We would be just fine without his ass and his bullshit I'm sorry gifts. I drove home in a fog. I can't remember shit I passed or thought about on my way there. My head was spinning and I was visibly upset, so my kids made themselves busy out of my space. They probably thought it was the grief making me angry… they had no clue and I wouldn't dare tell them. They would NEVER know them bastards as long as I was alive and if any motherfucka on this earth mumbled a word to my babies about that bitch babies my gun was gonna bust without warning or caution. Motherfuckas was gonna DIE. No discussion. That night I couldn't sleep, so I just laid on my sofa and cried. I was so hurt at what he did and the way he chose to tell me. He couldn't even be man enough to look me in my eyes while he was living and own up to his bullshit. Next thing I knew I was upstairs with these huge black trash bags emptying out his closet. By the time the kids woke up, the whole house was in disarray. I was trashing all memories of his ass. Clothes were everywhere, pictures and shit were broken. When they came downstairs I was sitting on the steps crying because at this point that was all I could do. I was hurt, angry, frustrated, confused, and scared. Every time I thought about it, I would start going through the motions again. And the fucked up thing was, if he hadn't died, this motherfucka would NEVER told me he had a WHOLE family on the other side of town. Then to make matters worse, Sissy and Mikey… two of the last motherfuckas on earth I wanted to see or speak to showed up at my house at 7 in the morning. I was too drained to argue so I sat quietly and let them speak their peace."

Keeli sits down on the opposite end of the sectional from Sissy and Mickey in the family room. Sissy takes a deep breath before she speaks. "Are you okay Keeli?"

"I've been better." Keeli snaps, unable to believe she actually asked her such a stupid question.

"Ke listen…" Mickey begins trying to explain what he could of the situation on his brother's behalf.

Keeli interrupts him before he can even get started. "No, you listen and listen good. I don't want to talk about it. He is dead and gone and it aint like I can confront him about it so just let the shit go. I have."

"I understand." Sissy says genuinely. "But Mr. Stienburg needs you to come by the office to sign the papers for you and the kid's inheritance."

"Oh that's not happening. I don't want that shit and neither do my kids."

"You playing right." Mikey ask in disbelief.

"Take a look around you Mikey, does it look like I'm playing?" Keeli snaps. "Take that shit and give it to his OTHER fucking family. My kids are fine. They don't need shit from his lying ass and neither do I."

"Keeli I understand you are upset…" Sissy begins

"Do you really!" Keeli snaps.

"Yes! I do! Why the hell you think me and Ian are divorced?"

Keeli smirks "I always thought it was because you are such a worrisome bitch."

Sissy takes a deep breath. "I will let you have that one because I know the pain you are in right now." Sissy walks over and sits next to Keeli as tears start to fall from Keeli's eyes. Sissy grabs her hand and holds it gently. "I know what Juan did was fucked up, but believe it or not Keeli, that man loved you with all he was. "

"Yeah?" Keeli questions. "Well I guess my love and y'all love is completely different because my love don't include a whole outside fucking family!"

"You are right chile." Sissy says in a defeated tone. "What I am trying to get you to understand is it is nothing we can do to change what has happened." Sissy begins to wipe tears of her own that have decided to show up to the party without her invitation. "I am learning Keeli, that life is far too short and unexpectant to dwell on things we can't change or control. Tomorrow is never promised to any of us chile."

"Ma is right Keeli. And besides all that, you have no idea what you about to give up. We saw the rest of that tape yo." Mickey tries to reason.

Keeli looks at Mickey, no longer even caring to wipe away her tears.

"And none of that shit will ever erase the pain he left me with from this bullshit." Keeli takes a deep breath to calm herself. "Look, I have a lot on my mind right now and I really just want to be alone."

"I understand." Sissy rubs her back soothingly. "I just want you to know that if you need anything, no matter what it is, you can call me."

"Sissy…" Keeli begins.

"No Keeli listen. I know things have been crazy between you and I. But we are still family. And we need each other to get through this."

"I know." Keeli says and wipes her eyes. "There is one thing I need. Can you take the kids today? I'm really in my own world trying to process this shit. I go back and forth with my emotions and I don't want them getting caught in the crossfire.

"Sure baby. Take all the time you need." Sissy assures her.

"I'ma take CiCi with me. It's been a minute since me and nephew hung out." Mickey says as he gets up and heads upstairs to let the kids know what's going on.

Sissy stands up and stretches. She looks around taking in the mess of a home Keeli's wrath has left behind. "Do you want me to help you clean up before we go?"

"No. Vye's coming today. She will handle it."

"Okay. I'm gonna go help Mickey get the kids together."

"Okay."

Sissy hugs Keeli. "And remember Keeli, I'm here for you."

"I know." Keeli replies as Sissy kisses her on the forehead before leaving the family room and heading upstairs.

"I didn't know what Sissy's angle was, but I was too emotionally and mentally drained to even try and find out. I mean, I knew this bitch hated me. She aided my husband in fucking around on me. She tried to have me thrown under the jail and even tried to coax him into leaving me. I knew she was full of shit with all that we are family mess she was singing. But at this point, I didn't have the energy to do shit about it.

I kissed my kids and told them I loved them as they went bouncing out the door with Sissy and Mickey. Once they left, I just laid on the sectional and cried. I felt so overwhelmed. It was hard for me to even breathe. The anger, the fear, the hurt, the sadness and THE GUILT of it all had me tied to the train tracks. Suicide kept crossing my mind. I couldn't function. Around 11am, Vye, our cleaning woman showed

***up and I was at what I thought was my lowest point. I was
ready to end it all. I couldn't take it anymore."***

Vye uses her keys to unlock the front door and comes into the house.
Keeli is sitting on the sectional crying uncontrollably with her desert
eagle on her lap. She is shaking uncontrollably. Vye stops on her tracks
when she sees her. "Keeli? Oh my God girl. What are you doing?" Vye
asks torn between shock and fear. Vye walks over to her. "Give me the
gun Keeli. You don't have to do this."

"No!" Keeli shouts. "Get away from me!" Just go Vye! Go the fuck on!"

"And let you kill yourself? I don't think so honey. What about your kids
Keeli? They need you."

"They have more than enough family that can take care of them." Keeli
reasons. "Just get the fuck on Vye! This doesn't concern you, so stop
trying to be a fucking hero!"

"It does concern me!" Vye takes a deep breath and sits down on the
ottoman. "Now I know I may be just the cleaning lady, but in the last two
years that I've been working for you and Juan, I started to feel like y'all
are my family. I care about you Keeli. I cared about Juan, and you know
damn well I love them babies like we share the same bloodline. So it aint
no way in hell, I'ma walk out that door and let you make the biggest
mistake of your life."

Keeli looks up and Vye and continues to cry. "I can't do this no more
Vye. It's my fault he's dead. My life is so fucked up right now. I'm no
good to nobody."

Vye eases over next to Keeli. She hugs her and Keeli begins to sob
uncontrollably on her shoulder. Vye eases the gun off Keeli's lap and
takes the clip out of it. She lays Keeli back on the sectional and puts a
blanket over her. "Come on Keeli. Just rest honey. It's okay to cry. It
will help you get some sleep."

"I can't sleep. I've tried Vye. I can't do anything right now."

"Hold on baby, I got something for you. It will help take the edge off."
Vye goes and gets her purse. She goes through it and pulls out a blank
pill bottle and opens it.

"What's that?"

"Just take it. When my mother passed, my niece got them for me. They
really helped me calm down and get through it.

"Okay." Keeli agrees with no more questions, wanting the pain to stop also.

Vye goes into the kitchen and gets Keeli a bottle of water. When she brings it back, Keeli takes the two pills and drinks the water. She lays there silently for about 10 minutes and then starts to drift off to sleep.

"When I laid there after I had swallowed those pills, I didn't know what to think or what the fuck was happening. It felt like I had to force myself to breathe, and my mouth felt so damn dry. I was gonna say something to Vye about what I was feeling but there was a part of me that was hoping those two grayish pills was about to take me to meet my maker. Next thing I knew it was the next afternoon. I woke up and I felt different. I wasn't tired anymore but I still felt pain. It was just my luck, Vye was there once again to hit me off. I was up for about an hour and then out of it again until the next day. The pain was still there. Vye told me my kids were coming home that day, so she only gave me one pill because I needed to stay awake. Before I knew it, I looked up and it was mid December and I had a full blown Oxi habit… now of course I didn't view it as a habit, but it was. I needed those gray pills just to get my ass out of the bed at this point in life.

Eventually, I finally made it back to Juan's attorney's office and signed the paper work I needed to sign for the kids and my inheritance. Juan left me his estate in Panama, his home on Billionaire's row in London and that's in addition to the home we brought out in Santa Monica and the one we were living in. He also left me two 747's, a yacht and 15 billion dollars cash. I was also now the sole owner of the three clubs we brought together. All of this was on top of what couldn't be mentioned in the will which was every red cent in the vault in our home.

To say I was set for life was an understatement….. yep an

understatement."

****

"I Am A Dope Fiend"

"In December, me and my family went to spend Christmas in Miami. Before we left, I paid Vye 3,000 dollars to get me a supply of Oxi. She came back with 60 pills and I was straight for the trip. A part of me felt like the pill popping was wrong but it really was helping me. I was able to function, to be a part of my kids life and most importantly, escape the reality of my husband being dead…. And having his blood on my hands. We spent 10 days in Miami and then came home. I opted not to go to my January prenatal appointment just as I had my December appointment. I knew my system was full of that shit, but I also "knew" my baby was fine. It wasn't like he was my first you know. So as long as I felt him moving around in there I didn't need to keep running to no fucking doctor.

When we got home from Miami, I made the decision that I was gonna sell the house we were living in out in Potomac, Maryland. It held too many painful memories. And every time I passed the spot where my husband took his final breath it haunted me to my soul. I couldn't keep putting myself through that. I felt like staying there was gonna make me either go crazy or OD, so I started shopping for a new home.

Vye had given me those 60 pills before we left and well that shit was GONE by the time I got back home. Yeah, I had a nasty habit. Her first day back to work was the day after New Years and I was itching for her to come through that door. I needed another hook up, and three grand was play money to me so I had 10,000 waiting for her to walk through the door because I wanted a triple score. 180 pills, and I wanted that shit like yesterday. But this time going, wasn't so easy."

Keeli is pacing back and forth from the living room to the family room looking out the window for Vye's car to pull up. Finally at 11:05am, Vye's Honda Accord pulls into the driveway. Keeli bolts from the family room and runs out the front door with no coat or shoes on. She runs down to Vye's car before she can get out. Vye looks up at Keeli standing in front of her in the January cold of Maryland in nothing but her nightgown and a pair of sweat pants. Vye instantly regrets trying to help Keeli by giving her pills. Vye signals for Keeli to back up with a shooing motion. Keeli backs up and Vye opens the door and steps out of the car. "Hey Ke, what's up." Vye asks, barely making eye contact with Keeli out of guilt.
"What's good Vye. Look I need a favor."
"What's up baby. And why you don't have no shoes and shit on Ke? You gonna catch a cold."
"I'm good, I'm good. Don't stress that. But I need you to go holla at your peoples."
"What you talking about?"
"I'm all out Vye."
"The fuck? Ke that was 60 pills, how the hell…"
"Look, I hooked my cousin and some folks up so that's why my shit gone. But we tryna get more. I need a triple score." Keeli goes in her sweat pants pocket and pulls out a bank envelope stuffed with cash and hands it to Vye. "That's 10 stacks right there Vye. Tell her I need 180, shit she can get me an even 200 for all them bills." Keeli laughs at her own sad joke.
Vye opens the envelope and thumbs through the money. She shakes her head sadly. "Keeli, my niece is in jail. She got knocked Saturday night writing bad checks and shit."
"You gotta be fucking kidding me."
"I wish I was."
Keeli leans against Vye's car and a defeated look crosses her face. "So you don't know nobody else who got that shit?"
"Nah. That shit aint easy to come by girl. It's all kinds of levels to getting

that shit on the street.

"What about whoever she be getting the shit from? I know she aint no doctor and shit. Not writing dummy checks and shit." Keeli snaps with an attitude.

"I wish I could help you Keeli but…"

"Yeah alright." Keeli snaps and snatches the bank envelope out of Vye's hand with an attitude. "You can bounce."

"What about the house?"

"The motherfucka aint dirty. I'll call you if I need you to come back." Keeli says as she walks away from Vye.

"Keeli, you know you can call me if you need somebody to talk to or anything. I understand. I've been where you are and I know how it hurts. I can help you."

"Man fuck you Vye. Can't nobody help me unless they gonna erase what the fuck me and my kids have went through. If you can't do that get the fuck on out my face with that help shit." She walks in the house and slams the front door. Vye gets into her car and leaves with a heavy guilty heart, feeling like she helped create the monster behind door number 1.

"I was so mad. I was so mad I couldn't even fucking see straight. What the fuck was I supposed to do. I was in PAIN or so I thought. My ass was really just going ill. But at that point in my life I couldn't or wouldn't see that shit. And this bitch talking about she knew how I felt. Her ass, like everybody else aint know shit. My husband was dead and his blood was on my hands. My step daughter was dead and her blood, just like her father's was on my hands. Until a motherfucka lived my reality, they couldn't understand where I had traveled to, why I was settling in here or how to help me leave this place of pure purgatory.

I NEEDED to get high. I knew that because I found myself crying and searching my house for something to take. ANYTHING that had narcotics in it. I checked ALL the bathrooms and found nothing I checked my room and there was nothing. I even checked all the kids rooms. All I managed to stumble upon was a half smoked blunt hidden in CiCi's sock drawer. I smelled it, I knew it was Reggie but at this point I gave no fucks and fired that shit right on up. I was in such a fucked up place in life, I was more pissed that this boy had me filling my lungs AND the lungs of his unborn sibling with some weak ass Reggie than I was at the fact that his ass was out here smoking weed. Yeah I was truly some shit.

When the blunt was gone, I spent about 30 minutes pacing and trying to figure out what the fuck was I gonna do because I was literally IN PAIN. Before I knew it I was on another seek and find mission. This time, my mission led me to the basement. When I opened the door that led to the lowest point in my house, I had no idea it also led to the lowest point in my LIFE.

Before I knew it, I was walking through the laundry room and then into "The Vault." Once I got in the vault, I realized wasn't shit in there but money. I turned to walk out and then it was like that monkey on my back said Bitch turn around. And it hit me like a ton of bricks...no pun intended. I still had 10 whole bricks of coke stashed in the basement. The shit had been there since the night I took it back from Donna more than a year ago. The night they told me about the spot getting hit. I went back into the laundry room, used all my dopefiend strength to push those two big ass stack dryers over. I felt around the wall until I found the faulty bricks. I pulled them out one by one until all 20 of them was stacked up on the floor and there it was. The treasure hidden inside the wall. 10 kilos of raw, uncut cocaine. I pulled out a brick and sat it on the folding table. Then I just stood there staring at that bitch for about 20 minutes.

I had an angel on one shoulder, a demon on the other and a fucking monkey on my back. And that demon and money was like tag team partners. They was wearing me down and my ass was already weak. Then my mind started drifting and I found myself thinking about Tiff and CoCo and how they got fucked up on that shit fast and hard. I was about to put that shit away and call Vye because I needed help, but them tag team partners was playing for keeps. They was in my ear telling me "You stronger than them bitches was." "You won't get hook like they did." "You just gonna do it this once to get by." Then the straw that broke the camel's back was dropped. They hit me with "If you don't do this, you probably gonna die from all this pain. Then them kids you love so much gonna be orphans. You already killed their father." I started to cry. I broke down in the floor sobbing and snotting. I was about to sell my soul to the devil to escape this pain. Then I heard the doorbell ringing repeatedly. I thought, this has to be my guardian angel. God sent someone over here to keep me from fucking up my life. I ran up the stairs so quick leaving everything where it was because I just needed to get the fuck away from temptation and open the door to the person who was saving my life without even knowing.

When I got to the front door, I was out of breath, I snatched it open and found a delivery man standing there. He was like "Delivery for Keeli Moreno." I signed quick and took the box. I opened it standing right there as he walked back to his truck. I opened the small box and inside was a stack of pictures. They were wrapped in a single piece of paper with writing on it. I unwrapped the pictures and read the paper. It simply said

Thanks a million. I couldn't have done it without you.

All the best,
Armend.

That's when I looked at the pictures and realized what I was looking at. It was pictures of Ti being raped and tortured. It was Juan and Randi as they left her apartment the night it all happened. It was their dead bodies mere seconds after the shooting. It was Ti in the ditch they left her in, It was me on the ground clutching my husbands lifeless body and crying. It was his twin brother Aleksander and him and Randi's son both hog tied and lastly it was them with clear bullets to their head. It was a strike to my already broken heart. I felt it was my fault the three of them were killed but to have this slimy motherfucka thank me for it hurt in ways I can't describe. I slid to the floor. Clutching those photos and cried until there was nothing else left in me. Everything came swirling back, The affair, the meeting with Armend, Randi trying to warn me and lastly the night they were taken from me. I don't remember getting up, closing the door, or going back to the basement but at some point I did these things. I found myself sitting at the folding table face to face with that brick. I grabbed a knife off one of the counting tables in the vault that we used to bust money wrappers and bust the brick open. Under the delusion that I was doing this to save my kids because I was so closed to dying from all the pain in my heart, I shaved off enough and created four fat ass lines and took my very first hit of raw, uncut, Colombian coke. And maaaaaannnnn them pills I had been popping aint have shit on what I had just put my hands on.

When I came up from my first line, my nose was burning like instantly. My vision was blurred and my eyes were watering like a sprinkler system. I felt like I was on cloud 9. I didn't have any worries, any pain or nothing else that would serve to fuck up my day. I did another line, and another and another. I sat there in a daze for about 40 fucking minutes straight. I didn't move. I didn't think. Fuck I don't even remember BREATHING. That's how gone I was.

This was the best I had felt since the morning my husband was killed.

I finally pulled myself together and put my new friend ways. I went upstairs to pee. I happened to glance in the mirror as I passed it on my way to the toilet and Rick James wasn't lying when he said cocaine was a hell of a drug. Apparently I had a nose bleed while I was spaced out. I had dried up blood on my nose and shirt. The high I was on was so ridiculously unbelievable to my body I hadn't even noticed that shit while it was happening. I chuckled at the sight and stripped naked to take a shower. When I stepped into the enclosed shower and the water started spraying from all angles, it felt so invigorating. Every single nerve I had was alive. When I began to wash my body, a familiar heat began to creep up my thighs and settle into my softest place. I was on fire and it needed to be put out. I began to explore my own body and while I was no stranger to masturbation, this time was different. I sucked my own nipples as my fingers worked overtime rubbing my clit until the pressure finally bust the pipes and I came with a scream. It was as if all the pent up anger and frustration was released with that orgasm. For the moment, I felt free. I melted to the shower floor and just let the steamy hot water fall upon my body. Once I was able to regain my composure, I showered properly then laid across my bed in nothing but my towel. I gazed at my wedding picture on the wall and the tears started to fall, but this time around they were happy tears. My mind was stuck on what felt like a home movie of my years with Juan. And all the bad shit had been removed. I cried joyful tears as every happy memory from the very first day we laid eyes on each other in Georgetown, til the last time we made love before he left my life came flooding my thoughts. I just laid there and cried, and laughed on my solo trip down memory lane until I finally drifted off to sleep.

That experience changed my life and well, that became my daily routine. Once the kids were out the door, I would head to the basements and do a line, or two or shit TEN and spend the rest of the day blocking out the bad, the hurt, the pain. I was happy again…. Or so I thought.

On February 14, I was rushed to the hospital in active labor. At 8:03pm, after a mere 2 hours of labor I gave birth to a 3lb 6oz baby boy. But this birth was far from the joyful occasion my other children's birth had been. I went into distress and had to have an emergency c-section. My baby wasn't breathing when he was snatched from my womb. There was no tiny cry to be heard and signal that all was well. I watched in a sober horror as they made several attempts to revive this tiny little life that was unsuccessful. His heart rate was dropping rapidly, so they wisked him out of the operating room because he needed more help than they could give him in that room. I was a wreck. Not being high, because well the first contractions blew that it for me had me here in the present instead of off in my head reliving the past. All I kept thinking was that this baby was not going to make it. I had killed him. It was no way he could have survived the cocaine war that was going on inside my body. My family was there and they were asking questions that I couldn't answer out of shame and a smidgen of denial. About 5 hours later, the doctor came to talk to me. I was so happy he asked my family to leave the room instead of just coming in blurting out shit.

He informed me that my son had high levels of cocaine in his system and it's a true miracle that he was alive. And in true junky form, I denied using. The doctor didn't even entertain my "This is some kind of mistake" pitch I pulled from way down deep in my ass. He informed me that my baby was stable for the moment but his hospital stay would certainly be long term if he made it through the night.

The day before I was released, the social worker came to see me and that was the very last thing I needed. She was following up on a report that was submitted by my doctor. I was informed that my blood showed extremely high levels of cocaine during the time I delivered. Overdose levels. And they would be launching a full investigation. Oh and the kicker was, instead of being released to go home, I was being arrested.

It had been 2 days since I gave birth to Sebastian Xavier Moreno, and truth be told I NEEDED to get home. My withdrawl wasn't that bad because I had a c-section so I was on percosets. It wasn't coke, but it helped me not go full ape shit and kill every hospital worker in sight. I needed to get home, and yes you already know why. But instead of returning to my fantasy world I was read my rights and cuffed right there in the room and taken off to jail....

AGAIN

The next morning I was in Family Court. The judge ordered me to submit blood, urine and hair follicles. I did and was held 3 days while shit was processed then we were back in court. Of course my shit was filthy and the charges of being under the influence of a controlled substance, child neglect, and child endangerment stood. My bail was set at 50,000 dollars. Ciaira paid my bail, and I couldn't even look at her as I walked out of the county jail. I had some serious explaining to do. Ciaira had been my bestie for years, and she knew I was holding a heart full of shame and regret. Instead of bombarding me with questions or judgement, she just held me and we stood there and cried together. I had really hit rock bottom.

We drove to her house in silence because I honestly didn't want to go back home ever. The next day, I had to face the music as my family wanted answers. I couldn't hide my shame as I told them the truth. I started out with Oxi because I couldn't deal with Juan's death, it lead to a nasty coke habit and now here we are. I was labeled an addict in the courts eyes, my newborn was sick and a ward of the state and I could have NO CONTACT with him until further notice. I sat in Ciaira's livingroom surrounded by her, my kids, my mother, my siblings and my God children and a few of my in-laws…. Mother-in-law included and I just cried. I was expecting judgement but my family rallied behind me and made it clear we were gonna get through this shit together. This wasn't my road to walk alone. I looked around that room and it finally made sense to me. All that money and shit I had was truly worth nothing. I was rich beyond measures with love, and that was more valuable than anything my money could buy.

It was time for some major changes in my life."

****

"A Brand New Kinda Me"

I stayed with Ciaira a few days but eventually I had to go home. I was thankful she decided to come with me the first few days because she knew as well as I did that although I hadn't powdered my nose since the day I went into labor with Sebastian, I was nowhere near being out of the woods yet. Yes I was a junkie in every sense. There had been times when I was at Ciaira house and I would go off by myself and cry like a fucking fool because I was truly ready to say fuck my entire family, all their support, my sick baby and everything else that should matter. I just wanted to run home and swim in coke, but my support system was on their shit.

By Dana having lived more than a decade as a junkie and then going through her own personal war to finally get clean, she knew I was far from out of the woods and she was my ROCK. She was there for the late at night phone calls when I felt my will to stay clean slipping away fast. And the day I went home, her and Ciaira was there to show me they meant business. They took me to that basement and I watched in horror as they dissolved 8 bricks of coke in the sink in the laundry room. Just sat the shit in there brick by brick and ran the water until it was no more. Maaaan I wanted to kill them bitches. It took a few hours for me to stop jonesing at the sight of all that work and focus on the fact that they were doing this to help me. So although my mother and bestie had committed grounds for fucking murder, I couldn't murder them.

Twice a week, Dana took me to my N.A meetings. I opted to go to the same place she was going. I didn't even know my mother went to meetings until then. I asked her why, cause she had been clean for years now and she told me that every day is a step, and some days she still stumbles and WANTS to get high… those meetings and the people she had come to know and love through them were her support when she tried to reason with herself that one more time wont hurt nobody. I felt out of place sitting there and listening to those people tell their tales. There was Katie, the white girl who was addicted to meth and hid her grandmothers passing for 3 years while she stole her identity and continued to cash her SSI checks so she could continue to get high. There was Raymond, who was addicted to crack, and was now alone in this world because he burned every bridge he ever had to get high. There was Krystal, who turned tricks to support her dope habit and ended up with HIV from sharing needles or sharing dicks. There was Michael who smoked so much weed he got high and left his 3 month old daughter in the car and she suffocated. Those were the few who stood out to me, and of course there was Dana. I learned so much about my mother's addiction from being in those meetings. All the years I walked around thinking she didn't give a fuck about the pain her addiction was causing us… her children. I never knew the pain my mother was suffering by being addicted. Now I understood. Because there was a strong part of me that knew this shit was wrong and knew my kids deserved better…. But sadly there was an even stronger part of me that just wanted to get high.

I went to meetings with my mother twice a week. Lamia took me to take my urines because they didn't want me to go anywhere by myself. CiCi got me a journal to write out my feelings and what I was going through in, and it really helped. It helped because if Monday was a bad day... I wrote about it. Every thought and every feeling. I did this, so when Friday hit, and it was a super bad day that I felt like I wasn't gonna make it through unless I got high... I could go back and read what I had already survived. And seeing what I had already survived vividly in my own words helped me to keep pushing forward. Shane also was a huge help. She found me a group for young widows At first, just like N.A I felt apprehensive about going to some damn meeting, but in the end I was glad I did go. It helped to know I wasn't alone in not being able to hear certain songs because it would remind me of the husband I lost. Or looking at my children and being so broken up because they looked just like their father. Or being angry because someone asked me how was I doing.... Like my husband fucking died, exactly how the fuck do you THINK I'm doing. It really helped to know I was not alone in all of this.

I also started seeing a therapist with my children. They had gone through a LOT lately. CiCi had lost both of his fathers and his sister.... And sadly he almost lost me. That was a lot on his young shoulders. So instead of seeing a therapist alone, I opted for family sessions because I needed my kids to come out of this storm okay. None of us would ever be the same, and I was wise enough to know that. But I didn't want my babies walking around holding in that pain for years to come and finding themselves fucked up as adults because this situation scarred them for life. So my weeks were busy as hell with meetings, urines, therapy sessions, writing for peace and writing for work and on Sundays I would get the whole gang together for dinner at my house, and that was after I would go to church with Sy. I'm not gonna lie, I wasn't fully sold on the religious aspect of things. But my sister came to me and asked me to just give it a try. And I did.

Like I said before I now realized what was truly important in this world.

I threw myself fully into both work and my family… legal work that is because I couldn't open myself up to that kind of temptation cocaine offered. I was an addict so I didn't even bother with the money or nothing because that money was only a step away from the drugs. I worked on two books for my company "Byrd Books" and threw myself into Bundy Entertainment, the company the nightclub were under. I would go into the office on Saturday mornings and Stay there all day. Sometimes, I didn't even have work to do but it was nice to just sit silently in the office I once shared with my husband. Our desk sat on opposite sides of our huge office on the 10th floor of the building we were housed in downtown. I would sit at my desk and think about all the times I would be over here working my ass off and he would sit across the room and do nothing but waste paper by balling it up and throwing it at me until I paid him attention. I remember the laughter that used to fill this office whenever he was here. I missed him so much. And while I spent those Saturday's at the office, Dana and my kids would go and see Sebastien. That eased my pain a little to know he would at least know a part of his family.

In April, I went back to court and since I had been 100 % compliant with the Judges orders My urines were dropped down to once a week and I was granted two hours of supervised visits with Sebastien per week. Some people would complain and say that aint shit, but to me, those two hours meant so much. I had taken that little boy through so much. I was the reason he would never know his father, I was the reason he damn near died, I was the reason he was addicted to cocaine, I was the reason he was a ward of the state. I was beyond thankful for the mere two hours I got to spend with him, and it wasn't easy. While it couldn't be diagnosed, the doctors were certain Sebastien suffered from neonatal abstinence syndrome. He cried all the time, he had issues feeding where the first two months of his life he ate via a feeding tube. He had sleeping issues and was sensitive to touch. Every time I was in his presence I felt like shit because I knew all the suffering his tiny body was experiencing was my burden to carry. I did this to him. And those doctors and nurses gave no fucks about WHY I chose to get high over the well being of my son as he lived in my womb. When I would come to visit, they gave no fucks about the millions of dollars I had, how Sebastien would never want for anything in life. They didn't care about nothing I could offer them. When I entered that Neonatal visiting room with the social worker and guard for my visits all they saw was junky. A well dressed junky, and truth be told, that's all I felt like.

At the beginning of July, I was back in court and this time the judge decided I had been in compliance long enough and Sebastien was allowed to come home. The goal was to get him home and the state of Maryland out of our business and we did that. Of course some palms had to be greased but hey.

I started to feel like I was finally making my climb back up from my fall from grace. I felt stronger than I had ever felt in life and I was ready to give up my crown in the streets. It wasn't worth it to me anymore on any scale. I had already made more money than my great-grand children would be able to spend in this lifetime. I had a good run, I had acquired some very profitable investments over time and business. I was worth billions and being as though I came from a welfare mommy sitting on the stoop dreaming on E Street to where I stood, man it was time to hang that shit up. I felt like if I continued, I was asking to find my ass in a 6x9 for the rest of my life. Ty had been doing his thing since the moment I took a step back, so it was no two ways about it. He deserved this shit. I decided I was gonna finish out the year as "CEO" and then I was GIVING my share of Bundy Enterprises in Colombia to Roc and giving the streets to Ty. This was gonna be their Christmas presents.

Two days after Sebastien came home, we set off to spend the rest of the summer abroad. Me, my kids, my immediate family and Ciaira and her kids went jet setting around the world. Shit me and my brats owned property we hadn't even seen before....shit in countries we had never stepped foot in, but being as though Juan was a man about the world, we now had it. So we went to check shit out. We all needed and deserved this vacation.

We spent two weeks in Panama and from there we trotted off to Spain. This was Asha and Sebastien's Estate. It was 10 minutes from the beach and on a clear evening, you could stand in the floor to ceiling windows of the master suite and see the place where the ocean and the sky collided. It was beautiful. I stood there every night and missed my husband til it hurt. From there, we visited Amsterdam and the last leg of our trip was to my enormous home on Billionaire's Row in London. As we pulled up we all sat with our mouths agape because this motherfucka was like nothing we had ever seen before. I don't even want to know why Juan had purchased the mini Buckingham Palace we were rolling into. This monstrosity consisted of 12 bedrooms, 13 bathrooms, a huge library that I could not wait to fill. It even had a separate staffing quarters where they could live and we would have nothing to do with each other after quitting time. The two weeks we spent there were indescribable. I decided on a whim that In January, me and the kids would live there. I announced my decision to my immediate family, Ciaira and her kids included and I offered them the opportunity to come with us. I told them all to just think about it, I wasn't coming back here until January anyway. Never in all the years I spent poor, broke, and a stones throw from homelessness did I think I would EVER be calling such a place home.

My life had truly changed. I lost a lot along the way, but I gained more than I ever dreamed of. When I got in this game, I was only foreseeing stepping my game up for my senior year in high school... stunting on a few bitches. I NEVER knew that the plan I made sitting on the block watching them niggas fuck the game all up would land me where I was now. I played the game and made it to the end. With that revelation I decided I wasn't even waiting until January to hand Roc and Ty the keys to the kingdom I build with my bare hands. I decided that the day we stepped foot back in DC, which was gonna be September 2nd, that was the day I would officially retire. They could have that shit. I was done.

I spent the rest of my vacation focusing on what was truly important to me. My family. On September 2nd, we left London as planned. We all boarded my private 747 headed back to the US. While I was relaxing on my plane with the closest people in the world to me, I had no idea of the grand surprise that was waiting for me to touch down. This was a homecoming I would never forget, no matter how hard I tried.

****

"People Change"

"We landed at Leesburg Executive Airport, the same place we always flew into. The ground crew came and greeted us as normal and began to unload the luggage. We started exiting the plane and the Chevy Suburban convoy that usually picked us up and dropped us off was waiting. We got settled in the trucks, our luggage was secured and it was business as usual. We started the ride back to my house in Potomac Maryland where everybody had parked at and such. We joked about the same thing we always joked about after one of our family vacations….. How we needed a vacation from our vacation because they were always amazing. When we got on the beltway, I noticed the convoy of Crown Vics kinda box us in. Before anybody could even utter a word about what we thought was happening, all suspicions were put to rest when the red and blue lights along with the sirens began blaring. The trucks we were riding in began to pull off to the shoulder and when I looked up I realized the Beltway had been shut down in both directions and we were being ascended upon by FBI, DEA and ATF agents. They had joint task forced my ass, so this here was not about to be no cakewalk for sure.

Blown, was too simple to describe how I was feeling, and extra is too calm to capture how these motherfuckas was performing out there. First what the fuck was they bothering me for? I had been out of the fucking country since July. What the fuck did they want?

Embarrassed as fuck was my mood as they literally SNATCHED our asses out the trucks, which was completely uncalled for. We were jetlagged, unarmed citizens and they were acting like we were fucking terrorist or some shit. They had us all, I mean my fucking kids and everybody handcuffed on the side of Interstate 495 looking foolish as fuck. They read us our rights and started carting everybody off to jail. Everybody who stepped off that plane had a fucking laundry list of charges from me all the way down to my Grandma Vickey. The shit was absurd. Everybody under 16 were taken to Social Services and everybody over 18 was taken to the Fairfax County Detention Center to be processed. My family members were being charged with conspiracy to traffic narcotics, Narcotics distribution and money laundering. I had those same three charges plus 16 counts of murder tacked on to my jacket. They had seized my home in Potomac and the home in Miami and all the contents of both. My plane was seized, the yachts, my bank accounts were frozen. The three clubs, and Byrd Books Corp. had been seized. If it had my name on it and occupied U.S soil, the Federal Government had their hands on it. If it had my mother's name, either of my sisters name, or my best friend Ciaira's name on it...... same stance. They even seized the U Store It in Riverdale, and I was praying to he who sits on high that it was empty. We saw a judge that night, they actually had one set up waiting to arraign us. They truly had their ducks in a row. And as you would guess, nobody got a bail set.

Their next step was to pull a Rayful on us. We didn't go to regular jail. They shipped us off to Quantico, to the fucking Marine base to be housed at. They had us all on lockdown for 23 hours a day. We had no contact with each other, or anybody else for that matter. This went on for two weeks. We ate alone, we slept alone, and the one hour we did get off lockdown daily, it was orchestrated so we would have absolutely no contact with each other. Not even able to see each other. I'm certain this was a part of their divide and conquer technique.

Finally after two weeks of this inhumane treatment, the joint task force was ready to talk to us. I know the plan was to let us stew in fear for a whole 14 days, and then motherfuckas would be ready to cut all kinds of deals and tell all. I had faith in my family, I had faith in my team. Fuck them was my tone and I knew it was the tone of my peoples.

They started their little interview process, and they made sure to save me for last. When it was time for my interview I was feeling some kind of way because I hadn't heard from Tia. It was no secret I needed her right now. The shit was all over the news and the newspaper. The first Headline I read was "Prominent business woman and soccer mom by day, Leader of a vicious drug cartel by night: The two lives of Keeli Nicholette Moreno. I read the article and was able to find out that the shake down wasn't just local. Apparently an undetermined number of members of the Notorious "QDC Mafia" throughout the United States were taken down. They had my high school year book picture next to a fucking mug shot. I was like wow, this is crazy. I found it interesting that I had been given TV access the night before I was called up for my interview, so I was able to watch a full segment of how fucked up me and my "gang" apparently were. And I was able to read the paper that morning during my breakfast. I guess this was another one of their weak ass tactics. Let me see how I'm being displayed in the media… what they already know so I would come in and cooperate.

Raspberries Bitches.

Wasn't nothing doing.

I had a mental talk with myself as I waited to meet with the joint task force because I had to make sure I controlled my emotions no matter what they put before me. Now was not the time for that hothead shit. I had to be the poised, calm and sophisticated lady that they say was all a front for the vicious drug lord that dwelled beneath my beautiful surface… the reporter's words, not mine. I was more than relieved when I got to the interview room and there was Tia. She stood to hug me, and I couldn't take my eyes off the man sitting behind her at the small table, sharp as cleats. Tia told me then she was just there as moral support, the man sitting at the table would be handling my case. She said Ian insisted the big guns get pulled out for this shit. I was star struck and glad Ian knew this wouldn't be easy. My attorney went by the name "J.C" and while I wont give you his name, he was responsible for getting an ex football legend off on charges of murking his wife… a white woman… in a highly publicized trial. And well everybody and their momma knew his black ass was guilty as sin. I guess Ian was thinking the same thing I was. If he could get his ass a walk on something like THAT, them folks might as well go on and open them gates and send me the fuck home. Stop wasting taxpayer dollars on bullshit. But let them tell it, they had a bird in the hand and this was the ONLY chance I was getting to speak with them before they buried my ass behind the wall for life, along with any and everybody who ever stood in the same room as me. My response was simple… BRING IT ON MOTHERFUCKAS!"

Keeli and Tia approach the table. J.C stands and greets Keeli with a handshake and they all take a seat at the table in the conference room. "How you been holding up?" Tia asks genuinely.

"I've been better." Keeli admits.
"Just keep your head up baby. It's all gonna be over soon." Tia adds with a warm smile. "This is…"
"No introduction needed. I know exactly who this is." Keeli offers trying not be so star stuck. "It's a pleasure to meet you."

"The pleasure is all mine." J.C offers.
"I wanted to take the case, but daddy insisted we pull out the big guns on this one. I hope that's okay with you."
"I'm cool with it. But you know I'm gonna need you for my family right?"

"I'm already on it. I've been to all their interviews. I think you'll be fine."

"I've reviewed the government's case against you Mrs. Moreno…" J.C starts to explain.

"Please, just call me Keeli."
"Okay Keeli. Their case is pretty weak, except for about 10 witnesses."
"Witnesses to what? I haven't done anything so how could they witness something?" Keeli offers actually sounding innocent.
J.C smiles at her maintaining her innocence. "Of the 96 people they rounded up supposedly members of QDC Mafia here in DC, ten of them have agreed to testify against you in exchange lesser sentences."
"That's interesting. But like I said, I'm innocent." Keeli lies.

"And I believe you." J.C counters with his own lie.

Just then, the three head agents of the joint task force, assembled to take down Keeli and her crew enter the conference room. Agent Carla Smith, a tall slender black woman with skin the color of midnight and flowing black hair that stops in the middle of her back takes the lead. "Good Day everyone. I'm agent Carla Smith of the FBI, also the lead agent on the joint task force that has dedicated their lives to you Mrs. Moreno." Agent Smith smiles at Keeli, taunting her. "This is Agent Fred Darnell of the DEA and Agent Anita Barnes of ATF."

"Pleased to make your acquaintance." J.C speaks for both himself and his client.

"Well at least we know you realize how serious this matter is. You sprang for J.C." Agent Smith jokes and the other agents chuckle."

"J.C, we have some very damning evidence against your client. Physical evidence, financial evidence, and most importantly, eye witnesses." Agent Darnell, A medium build white man, with Zack Morris from saved by the bell hair and ice blue eyes states and winks at Keeli.

"I'm almost certain that with all the shit stacked up against you, we could get a needle loaded up in your honor quick." Agent Barnes adds, staring at Keeli with narrowed eyes. Her wavy hair pulled back into a tight ponytail that looks like it's sure to give her a headache.

"What is your point Agent Barnes?" J.C asks.

Agent Smith stands up. "The point is, your client is looking at a life sentence at minimum if she is tried and convicted. So it's best to just talk to us now. Help us help you Mrs. Moreno." Agent Smith pleads with Keeli, offering her softened eyes.

"The only way y'all can help me is to toss these bullshit charges in the garbage and let me go home with my children." Keeli states in an emotionless tone.

"Mrs. Moreno, you call it bullshit but that's not gonna happen. We have hundreds of man hours of surveillance, and wiretaps." Agent Darnell explains. "That's not to mention all the physical evidence against you. And the eye witnesses."

"You see Keeli... Mind if I call you Keeli?" Agent Smith asks. "Your little crew wasn't as tight as you thought. Once a few of them heard the

type of time they are facing from fucking around with you, oh man."
Agent Smith laughs "You have no idea how many times we had to run
out to get more tape to record all that was being said."
"They literally gave us the game." Agent Darnell adds.
"Y'all are funny." Keeli chuckles.
"J.C, The United States Government is prepared to offer you client a
deal." Agent Smith says cheerfully. "We have permission to extend this
offer on behalf of the federal prosecutor…"

 "Not Necessary." Keeli interrupts in a tone just as cheerful as Agent
Smith's.

"You haven't even heard the offer yet!" Agent Barnes snaps, completely
annoyed with Keeli's smugness.
"I don't need to." Keeli says nonchalantly. "If y'all got so much
evidence against me, all these man hours of surveillance, all this physical
evidence, all these eye witnesses, then y'all got the game so why offer me
anything?"
"Mrs. Moreno, we know you are not the mastermind behind this cocaine
flood. The bodies, those are yours to eat, but what got everyone's
attention is the weight you've been moving." Agent Darnell speaks.
"According to a few of your codefendants, you have ties to Colombian
drug lords."
"Y'all get funnier by the second." Keeli chuckles.
"Plain and simple, we want the big fish Keeli. You are small potatoes."
Agent Barnes adds.

"Keeli, we know this is dangerous ground, but we are willing to offer you
protection." Agent Smith explains using a softer tone, hoping to reach
Keeli. "We can place you and your family in the Federal witness
protection program and…"
"Obviously y'all wasn't hearing me." Keeli finally speaks. "J.C, would
you please tell these federal clowns that I said fuck their deal. Let's go
ahead and go to trial. I aint done shit, so I aint worried about shit." Keeli
adds sweetly with a smile.
"You do realize this opportunity will not come around again?" Agent
Smith asks. "You either take this deal now, or next time you'll see us
will be in court."

"I'm just tryna figure out why the fuck you still here." Keeli laughs.
"Fine, have it your way." Agent Smith says with a hint of anger in her
voice. The three agents leave the room.

*"I wasn't even mad. I really just wanted to know who their so
called eyewitnesses were. J.C let me know that they were
gonna come hard now because I in so many words told them
fuck them, so say nothing to nobody if he wasn't there. He
aint have to tell me that shit because I had no words for
them. Just get me in front of a judge.*

*Three days later we were back in court for a bail review.
This time we lucked up and got a black judge. She seemed
annoyed with the Federal Prosecutor. She set bail for each of
my family members at 1.2 million dollars and mine was set
for an even 3 million. Lucky for me I had extended family
with looong money. The next day my bond was posted and I
was released with a petty ass ankle monitor. I was not
feeling this electronic leash shit… but it was better than
feeling that 23 and 1. I had to surrender my passports
immediately because the Federal Prosecutor said I was a true
blue flight risk. And I was, although I never thought about
running because I didn't wish to spend the rest of my life on
the lamb. But if I decided to, I could wind up anywhere. I
didn't fight it. I complied, and went to stay with Sissy because
that's where my children were.*

*The day after I got out, Sissy went and sprung my folks for
me because my hands were literally tied. All my accounts
were frozen and every piece of property I owned on U.S soil,
including my house in Potomac with the vault in the
basement was guarded 24/7 by armed federal agents.*

Once my family was sprung, Mikey gave up three of his investment properties for them to stay in temporarily because their homes and shit had been seized also. They set my trial for the upcoming January. So J.C and his team of associates had 4 months to get their ducks in a row while Tia and her associates worked out everything for my family aka my codefendants.

J.C got his witness list together on my behalf. His list included my financial planner and advisor who could clarify any so called issues the government seemed to have with my money. My business lawyers and accountants. He was gonna prove that everything seized had been paid for with legal motherfucking tender. I also had a list of character witnesses that included my kid's teachers, neighbors, and heads of charities I dealt with giving back. I wasn't worried about shit. I just wanted to know who those 10 witnesses were the government had, but they made that shit impossible.

The government kept all these bitch ass motherfuckas held without bond from September to January, and they kept the witness list sealed. They didn't allow J.C to interview them until a week before the trial was supposed to start. And the bad part about that was he wasn't even allowed to be in the same room with them. It was all done with cameras. JC would be in one room and they brought each snitching ass bitch into another room 1 by 1. Their faces were blacked out on the screen and their voices altered. All these talking ass bitches claimed they feared for their lives.

But it was still all good. It was on the government to prove my wrong doings and I knew that was a mission impossible I always covered my tracks. I was the Queen Of DC, I refused to be caught slipping."

****

"SNITCHES"

"When we arrived at the courthouse, that very cold first Monday morning in January, every damn news team in the business was occupying 3rd street watching for the Queen of what they were calling a real live black cartel to make her entrance into the Federal Court Building. Fox, NBC, CBS, ABC, News Channel 8, CNN, The Washington Post, Even New York Times reporters were braving a frigid cold to see your girl. I tripped out back in November when we got word that the trial was gonna run live on Court TV and A Buddy of J.C's who was a professor at Georgetown Law was using my trial as a part of his class. I went in back in November for a sit down with his team of budding can't wait to get that money defense attorneys in training. It was interesting. But my trial was gonna be a large part of their grade. Glad I could help the kids I guess.

The minute those black SUV's rolled up, cameras started snapping. You would've thought somebody famous for real was gonna be stepping out but it was just little ole me….. Keeli from the block.

I felt amazing as I went stepping up in that federal courthouse. I was killing them in a pair of exclusive Christian Louboutin's. I wore a black asymmetrical Yves St. Laurent dress that I brought while in Paris and I topped it off with a black military style YSL coat. The price tag on my outfit was outrageous. And I rocked a 25,000 dollar custom made platinum and diamond tiara on my head to show these motherfuckas. A lot of folks would've been trying to be humble and shit, appeal to the jury, be somebody they not to get their ass out of the sling but not I. All I knew how to be was me. Keeli Nicholette Byrd-Moreno. No Humble. All hustle, all heart.

From January 3rd until January 24th, the federal prosecutor and her team had the floor and did their thing. They had maaaadddd photos of me meeting with Ty on several occasion where we would be standing and talking and then he'd transfer duffle bags from his trunk to mine then I would be on my way.   I'm like fuck that could've been anything in them bags, maybe I was doing Ty laundry or some shit for all they knew. They had pictures up of the areas I controlled in DC then they showed pictures of that coke white wall, their initial bust…. What actually landed my ass in the hot seat.

Apparently, what had happened was… and maaan you not even gonna believe this shit. Do you remember back when Ciaira got that letter from BJ and we were supposed to go see him, but never got around to it? Yeah, well apparently that pissed him off. So he got in touch with Shameeka dumb ass and had her coming to see him. Now not only was she seeing him, but he was using the sharpest knife in the fucking drawer to smuggle coke FROM MY SUPPLY into a federal fucking prison. I mean really, how fucking stupid could you be? This shit lasted only a few months from like October to January and then her dumb ass got busted.

So the weekend that all hell broke loose, when my spot was getting hit and them bitches was at the Go-Go. When I was meeting with everybody and Shameeka ass wasn't nowhere to be found, that's because she was busy getting caught trying to stuff coke she smuggled into her smelly twat into tissue rolls in the women's bathroom. The person who was on clean-up duty was BJ peoples and was supposed to collect that shit later after visits when he was allowed to clean the women's bathroom. Well some woman went in after Shameeka and discovered the coke because she hates public restrooms and tissue that everybody done fucked with. So she grabs one of the extra new ones that they keep stacked in the bathroom and unwraps it and boom, a whole bundle falls out on the floor. She freaks and is afraid she may get arrested for it and runs out and tells the C.O. They come investigate the shit and lock the entire prison down. Visitors especially can't leave because it's a civilian bathroom so they know this shit came from the outside. They run back the tapes, and get this it was clear who stashed it. Shameeka was there on the very first visit and she was the only person who had entered that bathroom before the woman who found the coke. When the corrections officer was on the stand telling this story, I wanted to fucking scream. This bitch was ass backwards. EVERYBODY know you don't pull no shit like that 5 minutes into no visit just in case some shit like this happen. And it wasn't hard for them people to know who she was smuggling the shit in for because well, she was on his visiting list and had been coming to visit him for months now. They had them dead to rights. Now BJ ass already had 70 years he copped to. HE WAS NOT COMING HOME point blank. So he could've easily owned up to the dumb shit they was doing and him and Shameeka just do their fucking time like you supposed to do, but nooooo. This nigga was in his feelings about me and Ciaira being out here living life and shit and the fact that the life we were living got in the way of us coming to see his ass so he flat out lied and told them people he was doing this shit on my behalf, and Shameeka disloyal stupid ass went right along with it. So they started running their mouths and next thing you know a whole joint task force is built in my honor.

Now aint that sweet.

Their first idea was to put an agent in my crew back in that March, but BJ and Shameeka, like the true bitches they were gave them the game. They told them it wouldn't work because I wasn't stupid by far and wasn't going for it. If I didn't know the person, I wasn't fucking with them. So since that plan wasn't gonna work, they chilled and kept getting fed info by BJ and Shameeka. Shameeka let them know that Ty was running shit because I considered my own self HOT and wouldn't touch the dope because of my charge back in January. So they thought they was gonna take a run at Ty but she also told them Ty wasn't fucking with nobody without my ok stamp. So they waited.

They waited until Shameeka TOLD THEM me and Ciaira were over in Milan and put their plan into action.

Enter Agent Damien O'hare known to the streets as Krazie.

Over the months, Shameeka had been acting like everything was everything and had been talking to Ty every chance she got talking up her peoples named Krazie. When I left the country, she introduced them and they instantly clicked. Which wasn't hard because Shameeka fed this nigga everything he needed to know to appeal to Ty and it worked like a charm. I guess Ty ass had been lonely for a bestie since Jon-Jon died all those years ago.

The plan was to get Krazie good in with Ty, then when I came home they figured Ty would introduce him to me and since Ty was vouching for him, I'd welcome him with open arms and then literally make their case for them, but of course shit aint even play out like that.

Ty KNEW if I found out that he brought somebody into my organization without my say so he would've been dead on sight. I didn't give a fuck how close we were. True enough I loved Ty like a brother but I wasn't for the bullshit. When you wrong, you wrong point blank. I wouldn't have given two blue fucks how much Ty was vouching for that nigga. I wasn't fucking with him. If anything I would have ended up with a needle in my arm for assassinating a fed. So I guess I should thank Ty for never letting me in on the secret. Them feds really thought I was some ole goofy bitch that was just gonna go for whatever shit that put in my line of vision. Boy were they wrong.

So like I was saying, to cover his own ass, Ty NEVER breathed a word about this nigga Krazie to me. Also when I came back, I left everything as it was with Ty running the show. So they still couldn't touch me. They just kept on with their surveillance and shit. They kept that running right along with BJ and Shameeka's mouth. And now at least in my eyes, Ty ass was telling too. Okay officially he wasn't BUT he was fucking with this nigga Krazie and telling him shit and Krazie was adding it all to the files. Then back in September, while me and my family were winding down our world tour and getting ready to come back home, Ty dumb ass decides that he gonna take this My Buddy ass nigga to Arizona with him.

All I could do was shake my own damn head as I listened to this clusterfuck unfold. Like really Ty. You GAVE these motherfuckas their case in every sense of the word.

The feds let them pick up and bring 2400 Kilos of pure

Colombian coke all they back to DC and busted their ass then. They pulled a synchronized sweep and started snatching up everybody and waited ever so patiently for my flight to land. Now being that Ty dumb ass took a federal agent with him to the Arizona/Mexico border to pick up a shit load of coke, they now wanted to know who I was fucking with so that's why they was all like we can protect you blah blah blah just tell up who got that dope.

Fuckouttahere

So their synchronized Nationwide snatch up netted them all kids of big fish. They got the whole entire home team, "Baltimore Slim", my peoples up in New York, Trenton, Philly, Cincinnati, Miami, Jacksonville, Tallahassee, Monticello, Atlanta, Savannah, Boston, Chicago, New Orleans, St. Louis, Vegas, Nashville and Jackson Mississippi. After they sorted through the bullshit that two weeks that had my ass sitting on ice, I had a list of codefendants that was 506 names strong. A large majority of them folks I didn't even know. They was folks that worked for or fucked with folks I fucked with. Of the 506 names, 96 of them came from my home team. Motherfuckas who I personally dealt with out my city. Niggas and bitches who I essentially wrote their fucking paychecks.

Some walked, some cut deals and some did exactly what you supposed to do if you find yourself in the hotbox. Shut the fuck up and go'n do ya time. I liked to had fell out when I realized they had gone all the way back in my past and drug Monae ass into this shit. Not on no charges for all the dope she help me flood the streets with but as a State Witness. I was feeling some type of way when this bitch hopped up on the stand doing the same shit that got her ass exiled to begin with…running her fucking mouth. I was even more in my feelings because when we put my fucking blood in the ground, this bitch was there. Her coming back around at a fucked up time in my life made me welcome her back in my life as my sister. Me and Monae had been talking almost every single day. She had sat her funky ass up in my home, hugged my kids, she even wiped my eyes and told me I was gonna be okay when I lost the love of my life. And to know all that shit was fake. All that shit was so she could get close to me cause she was fucking with them peoples. I wanted to say fuck the bullshit and kill that bitch right in the court room and just take whatever time they handed me. But she wasn't the only one I had to force myself to remain unbothered by.

Of them 96 motherfuckas from the home team that got nabbed, 10 flipped. I was damn near ready to blow each time one of them took the stand to snitch. These was motherfuckas I held at a higher regard sitting there ratting me out. Folks who I clothed and fed was up in there running their mouth like nobodies business. The same motherfuckas who would be dirt broke and fucked up if I hadn't taken them under my wing was now on some tattle tell shit.

The snitch list started with BJ, and that hurt like hell to watch. This nigga was my family. My blood. FIRST COUSIN. Like seriously his mammy came out the same hole as my daddy. This nigga put me on, taught me everything I knew and now he was staring at me with pure malice in his eyes and larceny in his heart. His testimony was the only one I got emotional for because I loved this nigga like nobodies business. He was like the big brother I never had, so how could he do me so wrong. It wasn't like I didn't come to see him cause I aint give a fuck, I never made it out there because I was going through shit myself. This nigga knew he was never coming home so he held back no detail. I mean

NONE. Even down to me wanting to hit Detective Bell when he started extorting me. And that opened the door to what happened to him. The prosecutor immediately went into the news clippings that told the story of Detective Bell being a dirty cop and being killed in a drug deal gone bad. BJ told them while I never told him I did it, he knew I did because I was so adamant about hitting him. By time he left the stand, disgust was too light to describe what I felt for him. He even told them folks that I hit his baby mother and ex right hand because they set him up. I was numb after his testimony. My own family wanted me with a needle in my arm. So with my family being this shady, I wasn't surprised at by nobody else who to the stand. Okay well I was surprised as to who they were because again the witness list was sealed. So it wasn't until I saw them sitting on the stand being sworn in that I knew who they were. Shameeka, Monae, Donna and Ty. The other five were really nobodies so the shit they told was mostly hearsay and shit they thought they knew. But that other five. Yeah, they gave them the game word for word.

By time these motherfuckas got finished talking them people knew all about my issues with Daye… so of course now they were looking at me for his murder also. Donna told them about the night in the salon. Monae told them how we got started, how she got kicked out and witnessing the murder of Kia's sisters. Ty told them all about the night Jon-Jon, Re-Re and the Officer got killed at the Burger King. He also closed the cases on them bodies at the trailer park that night. He finished up the story on what happened to Detective Bell and his peoples including Magdelana. The body count was adding up something hefty.

The night after Ty testified, I found out something even more interesting from Tia. I never knew Magadelana was Ian's niece. She had been exiled from the family when she started fucking with Bell. Ian told me under normal circumstances I would be dead, but being as though she was not considered family at the time of her death AND she was fucking a nigga who tried to get his son a life sentence, I got a pass.   I didn't say it, but at that moment, I was glad Juan was dead, because once the trial was over I planned to put as much distance between myself and his family as possible. I had to. With what Ian had told me about Magdelana, I knew if it ever came out that me meeting that nigga in Milan is the reason why Juan died, they would kill everybody I ever knew. So I took it for what it was worth, and mentally started cutting ties with them all.

By time the prosecution rested, they was even tryna put the deaths of my own sister, cousin and my son father on me. Good thing I was in Miami at the time and had a million motherfuckas who could legitimately vouch for that.

J.C did his thing ripping into the asses of each and every one of the prosecutor's witnesses. Like he was telling the jury, they basically want you to take the word of a bunch of admitted drug dealers, liars and killers that the only person name on the docket who was never apprehended in the same zipcode with one ounce of coke, one smoking gun, one bullet, or one dirty damn dollar is a drug dealer, liar and killer. And that was true. The fact that they admitted what they had done in the process of telling on me was a slap to their credibility if you ask me. Other than pictures of me meeting with Ty and getting some duffle bags they had nothing on me. Like NOTHING.

When the prosecution rested and the defense began to do their thang, I just sat back, adjusted my crown and smiled. J.C had a witness list of respectable motherfuckas I dealt with outside of the street that painted a totally different picture than that pack of criminals before them. With the defense witnesses, the jury was made aware of all my charity work, the youth outreach centers that I founded nationwide…. Not in my name because I wasn't looking for publicity, just doing my part to stop other children from facing any of the things I once faced. While my name sat on not one building, saying I did this, it was on every financial document tied to the organization because I did that shit with my own money. I wasn't lobbying shit from the government or nobody else. I did that. There was a lot of talk about the jobs my companies generated. The scholarships I had given out. All the positive shit about me the government cared not to know anything about was out front and center. J.C told them I was just fortunate enough to marry a Colombian business man who made sure I was 100% well off before his untimely demise and after. They had a bunch of criminals speaking for them and I had a bunch of upstanding citizens speaking for me. So you do the math.

The defense wrapped up on February 11th and on the 14th closing arguments took place and the jury was dismissed to deliberate. The Jury deliberated from the 15th til 18th. At 5:30 that Friday evening we got the call that the Jury had reached a verdict but it wouldn't be announced until Monday. On Monday February 22nd, we were back in court. The press was ready, I was ready, the world was ready to hear my fate.

The judge gave a short speech and then asked the jury foreman if they had reached a verdict. The tall white woman with blonde hair and blue eyes who had been chosen to be the talking head peace by the jury that was supposedly of my peers that consisted of 5 Blacks, 4 Whites, 1 Asian, and 2 Hispanics…… 7 women and 5 men, stood up and took a deep breathe before reading the verdict that shook the entire federal courthouse.

Not Guilty on all counts.

I didn't make a sound, just smiled and hugged J.C. My family was live as fuck tho hearing that shit. It took 20 minutes for the judge to calm down the courtroom.

The judge said a few more words that nobody truly gave two fucks about, thanked the jury for their service and then dismissed their asses. Next she announced I was a free woman and ordered the feds to get their grubby overzealous hands the fuck off my shit IMMEDIATELY. I laughed my ass off as I looked over and saw the anger in the prosecutors face, along with the heads of her task force and every other dumb fuck who had spent a second working what they all figured was a career case, and it was…. A true career case, just not the way they were hoping. I'm positive asses would be had and badges snatched the fuck off chest before the end of the day. I blew kisses at their asses as we excited the courtroom and they actually had to hold Agent Barnes back because I flipped that bitch the bird and she lost her everlasting fucking mind and charged at me screaming bitch it aint over. She was really fucked up I was not on my way to nobodies 6x9…. But back home to a house she could never afford and cars she could only dream about driving.

When we stepped outside, 3ʳᵈ street was shut down due to all the traffic as far as the media, and people who just wanted to get a real live look at the bitch who took DC by storm, turned that shit upside down and then laughed in the feds face. Me and J.C gave a brief press conference on the steps of the courthouse. Well he did, because the same way I never opened my mouth in that courtroom, I wasn't opening it now. As I always said, what's understood needs no discussion.

Two days after I walked, the charges against my family were dropped. I mean if you couldn't get me, the actual guilty one, how the fuck was you gonna get the innocent ones? J.C was paid a substantial amount of money for all his hard work and he went on about his business. I was just glad it was all over. The funny shit was J.C wanted me to take the stand in my defense during the trial but like I told him, under no circumstances do I talk to police not even to defend myself. That was that bullshit. You start out talking to defend yourself, next thing you know its 100 hours later, you still in the box, they still grilling you and now switching your words around, but you so mentally drained you don't peep game and then you find yourself sounding like Kane on Menance mumbling some shit about what time you brought the beer and shit.

No Bueno

Silence is golden when fucking with them peoples.

Once that shit was officially over with, so was my illegal business dealings. It just wasn't worth it anymore. That trial had showed me so much, how even motherfuckas I would've gave my life for out in them streets like BJ and Ty gave not one single fuck about me when it all boiled down to it. And it's crazy because I was literally about to gift wrap a crown for Ty when I touched down and make that nigga the King of the Streets… and his bitch ass told on me. I still couldn't believe him and BJ. Every time I thought about that shit, I got angry… but then I thought about those words NOT GUILTY and couldn't help but smile. Now that shit was music to my ears, even though I knew what the outcome was gonna be from day one. The only evidence they had was me collecting duffle bags from Ty bitch ass on a couple of occasions, and the testimony of 10 admitted felons. No guns, no weapons of any kind, no coke in my hands…. They couldn't even put me in the same fucking zipcode as all the coke they said I was moving so sorry task force motherfuckas. NO BUENO.

But since that shit is a thing of the past, Imma go ahead and give yall the game. Y'all should've already known though. We wasn't leaving shit to chance. My extended family put the whole jury on notice that they could be and would be touched if they aint play that shit by OUR playbook. I mean it's real easy to get motherfuckas to see what you want them to see when you got wives, children, brothers, sisters, husbands, fuck even pets walking around with targets on their backs every single day of the trial. When it was all said and done, since they played fair, they each got hit off with a mil ticket. And the judge that was presiding over the case got two million, so my ass was gonna walk regardless. Even if one of my victims left the grave and wiggled up in the courtroom and told them It was Mrs. Moreno, in the den with the candlesticks the jury would've still been like…..

FUCKOUTTAHERE!

And just so we clear, J.C had absolutely nothing to do with the jury tampering. That was soley the work of Ian and the family, because truth be told had we left that shit up to chance my ass would probably be UNDER the fucking jail now.

In a way, I guess I could have thanked the tattle tell crew for running their mouths. Because shit kinda got crazy what felt like the minute I walked out that courthouse a free woman. That trial garnered me a ton of publicity. My clothing line was moving quicker than my coke did all them years and you know that shit was moving at lightening speed. Once I reopened my clubs, them bitches was at capacity each and every night, and when I released my first book "Trap Star" in April, that bitch shot straight to number one. It was based on my life and well, motherfuckas wanted to know how I did what I did the way I did for as long as I did. They wanted that blueprint and I gave it to their ass so to speak. My phones were ringing off the hook with everybody trying to get an interview or get me to appear on some talk show and shit, but that wasn't me. I was chilling. Other motherfuckas hustled to be seen, I hustled to disappear. And well shit got so bad I had to do just that. I was focused on spending time with my kids and just tryna put that life behind me, but the fake paparazzi wouldn't let me be. I'm talking about staking out my kids school, trying to give me cash for an exclusive, trying to even talk to my kids. It was all too much so by April I had to pull them out of school and have them homeschooled just so we could maintain our privacy."

****

" *At Last, I am Free*"

"In May, I took my kids and a few very close family members and we went back to London. We stayed there until Labor Day once again, lounging on Billionaire's row enjoy the wealth. I figured by time we headed back to the States the media frenzy would have subsided and we could get back to life. I have to admit, being in London, I felt at peace. I felt happy and that was an emotion I truly hadn't felt in a long time. I had my health, I had all my kids and my ass wasn't in jail. I felt complete. I didn't have a man of course because Juan was dead and gone, but you know what, after all the bullshit he had taken my heart through I was fine laying down by myself at night and waking up the same way. I couldn't be anything but happy. If I had lost everything in the blink of an eye and had to go back to being regular ole Keeli on the block… the same bitch I was in 1993, I would've found solace in that at this point…… nah I'm fucking with you. I probably would've jumped off the porch one more gin just a bit wiser.

Over the summer, I wrote my second book titled "Tattle Tell: Dedicated To All The Fake Motherfuckas In The World" yep, just like that. It was about my codefendants that chose to run their mouths instead of stick to the script. Yeah, I can't even lie, I was still maaaadddd salty behind that shit. These was my peoples. Motherfuckas who had put their feet on my couch before went down there and tried to get a needle in my arm. I was so mad I wrote that motherfucka in two weeks flat. It dropped in August and that bitch was doing Harry Potter numbers by the time we headed back to the states.

When we flew back, we landed at Leesburg as we always did and from the moment my feet touched the ground, I felt out of place. Being back in the place I called home all my life just didn't feel like home to me anymore. Too much had happened for shit to be the same. I had lost too much on the streets of DC to still wave my two striped, three starred flag in the air. It was time to free myself.

I didn't see the point of putting the kids in school when I was planning to be out, so they stuck with homeschooling from September until January. By January we were packed up and ready to officially say goodbye to the DMV. I sold the house in Potomac, the same house where I kissed my husband for the last time. I brought a beautiful stone home in the elite estate of Old Preston Hollow down in Dallas Texas. It was one of those home you just stared at and thought damn. It was amazing from door to door and from floor to ceiling. My kids loved it, and I loved it and my family loved that we did not go jumping back over that damn pond to London.

In March, I threw myself a huge birthday party in Miami. Me and my kids went down a week before to get things together. Ciaira kept telling me she had a huge surprise for me and I couldn't even imagine what it was until I came running out my front door in nothing but a pair of cut off shorts and a tank top to greet her and my God babies. I hadn't seen them since we all came back from London. Me and Ciaira talked twice a week faithfully and she kept saying she had a surprise for me. When her and the kids hopped out of the Suburban she drove I could see it was two other people in the truck. The first one stepped out and I didn't know who the hell he was. He stood about 6'3, darkskin and buffed. I started thinking, I know damn well she aint bringing me no skripper or no shit like that. Then he grabbed her hand in a loving tone and I knew he was only skripping for her ass. But the next person who stepped out the truck immediately took my breath away. He still looked the same as he did when I was a mere 12 year old little girl running with Ciaira, scribbling his name on my notebook. My very first love. Her cousin Frederick.

Fred had always been the one who got away in my eyes. I met Fred when I was 12 and he was 16. He was out there on the block getting his money but that wasn't what pulled me into him. His smile captured my heart the first time I met him all those years ago. He said hello, and my palms started sweating, the butterflies started fluttering and my voice became a whisper as I spoke back, completely under his spell. He smiled at my reaction, and I just wanted to be his. From my understanding he was digging me too but there was the fact that I was 12 and he was 16 going on 26. We talked on the phone every now and again, I started to feel like it was only when he was bored because he knew I wanted him, but he never made a true move for me. We met the summer of 1987, and by the fall he was gone. He was truly ahead of his time and I understood why he really never made a play for me. It wasn't until he caught a double murder charge that I understood how big the gap between me and him was back then. We wrote each other while he was in jail up until the time I met Jackie and then things kinda drifted apart. I had never even kissed this man but I knew that I loved him. Ciaira had been keeping in touch with him since he came home. And apparently when she said she was coming to see me he was like fuck that lets hit the highway. It had been all of 100 years since we had seen each other, but I swear the minute he stepped out that truck he took my breath away again. I don't know what came over me, but I took off running and leapt into his arms. He caught me and kissed me like he had been waiting for that kiss his whole damn life. I felt so safe in his arms. I never wanted him to put me down. I remember a long time ago when me and my Grandma Wanda was talking and she told me "If a man gives you butterflies and makes your heart all a flutter, he's fine for awhile but he aint the one. But if a man holds you in his arms and you feel safe... you feel protected... you feel loved, then baby THAT'S HIM. The crazy thing was we had this conversation for the last time about 2 days before I married Juan. I think that was her subtle way of telling me that he wasn't for me. I didn't pay it no mind until the moment I was in Fred arms. It all made sense, it all felt right.

That night, after everyone else was asleep, me and Fred were sitting out on the wrap around porch talking…. Just playing catch up because we had A LOT to catch up on. He leaned in and kissed me in a way that told me he knew my inner most desires at that moment, and it was him. It was crazy how it happened, but we made love right there on my porch. We were on the side of the house so being seen by a neighbor or anything wasn't a concern. I had been fucked outside before, but this night was different. It was something in every stroke, in every kiss, in every whisper that we shared that made me forget about everything from my past. Fred took me to a place where Juan and the hurt he brought into my life no longer mattered, where Jackie didn't matter, where Simm didn't matter. It was just me and him. Before I knew it, I was crying. Not a sad cry, but a happy cry because I knew I had finally found him. I found my other half. The man I was meant for and the man who was meant for me. When it was over, we just cuddled in each other's arms on the patio sofa with a blanket and we stayed and watched the sunrise.

The week went by far too fast, before I knew it, it was time for my birthday celebration which was amazing and then everybody was heading home. Fred told me straight up that he wanted me and wanted to be with me. I told him I wanted him too and with that, he didn't go back to DC. He said fuck everything for me and came back to Texas to be with me and I couldn't have been happier. On New Year's Eve he proposed to me and I said yes with the quickness. On February 14th, me and him stood together on a lonely hilltop in Hawaii with just the preacher and my kids as our witnesses and said our I Do's. I didn't need the big excessive wedding, and Fred was a low key kinda dude where he didn't need to be seen. So we were good. Some people may have thought Fred had ulterior motives for asking me to marry him but he didn't. He told me he fell in love with little ole Keeli from the Block a long time ago, but my age stood in our way…. Then his jail time… but he never stopped wanting me. He even went and had a prenupt drawn up saying if by some snowballs chance in hell we didn't make it, he would leave simply with what he came in with. Not that I was worried about that, because I would've killed his ass before I let him drain me anyway. Love or no love.

I have to honestly say, I had never been as happy as I was at that point. There was no drugs, no fighting, no cheating, no stress…. Just love in my life in all areas and damnit I deserved it.

A year after me and Fred got married, Ciaira married her dude Keith and they moved to Paris. Ciaira was so heavy in the fashion scene she had to be at the heart of the shit. The day she left, me and her both cried like babies. We were at the airport and she told me thank you. She said she often thought back to that day in 1993 when I sold her a dream and made it come true. I believe in all the time I got it how I lived and all the people I helped and looked out for, Ciaira was the only person who ever gave a genuine "Thank You". That was all I needed.

That following fall, I had to say goodbye to someone else who meant so much to me.

My mother.

Dana never told anybody until she found herself in the hospital fighting pneumonia which is what ultimately killed her. My mother had been living with HIV for years. She said she found out she was positive right around the time found out I was pregnant with the twins. She said she didn't tell us because she didn't want us to throw her no pity party. We were happy as a family and she wanted us to stay that way. I sat in that room and held my mother's hand and listen to her tell me how she always loved me, even when she didn't know how to show it. She apologized for the times she left me feeling like I had no one and having to face the world on my own. I cried with her and told her I forgave her a long time ago. And I told her how I appreciate how stellar of a grandmother she had been to my children. In my eyes that made up for everything me and her had personally gone through. The last thing my mother told me was that she was happy to have finally been able to see me happy. And like I said, I truly was. She told me she was at peace now and then she went on to rest. I sat and cried by myself because I was both sad and happy. I was sad that my mother was gone, but I was happy because I had a shitload of amazing memories me and her had been able to create despite the past. And I would use those memories to help me smile when the days of missing her became too much.

The last I heard of Donna and the snitch crew is they were still in jail. In 2008, sadly BJ killed himself in jail. I guess the snitch jacket got to be too damn heavy for him. I went to his funeral, even Ciaira and little Byron came over and went to his funeral. Ciaira and Little Byron came because well that was his dad and at one point he was her other half. I went because even though I was fucked up with him, I still loved my cousin. I mean shit if it wasn't for him, who knows where my ass would be. And I wanted him to have peace. I needed his spirit to know I held no anger or malice in my heart for him even after he did me dirty. Fred said that could have been the reason why he did it. Because even though he sold me out and tried to get me a needle in my arm, I still kept his books stacked, as I always did even before he sold me out because he was my family. And even though he fucked me over, I still loved him. Honestly though, sitting in that church during BJ's funeral wasn't the thing that hurt the most. What hurt the most was being 10 feet from my father and him refusing to even acknowledge me being there. He didn't even bother to come to my mother's funeral. I wanted to talk to him because life was short, I had already lost my mother and now he was all that I had as far as where I came from. And knowing that he hated me so much did something to my spirit. The same way he lost his daughter, I lost my sister and that still hurt. Why couldn't he see that I was his daughter too and damnit I needed him now more than ever? I don't know if he couldn't see it or wouldn't see it. But I didn't push. I gave him his space to forget about me once again.

I went back home after BJ's funeral and poured myself into writing, publishing and keeping Byrd Books rocking. Fred took over the clubs for me and added 5 more to our portfolio in Dallas, Houston, Las Vegas, L.A, and San Diego. My kids turned out to do well even though they were born into a toxic mix that could've had them fucked up for life. None of them got on no fly shit because they were caked up. They liked the idea of getting up in the morning and running million dollar companies. I guess they got that hustle hard even when you got it aspect from their momma.

I was more than surprised when I got a call from my aunt Maxine out the blue telling me an arrest had been made in CoCo's murder. Apparently, Simm turned himself in. He said they were haunting him and he finally came clean on everything. I flew back to DC because I wanted to be there for his sentencing. He didn't have a trial since he pleaded guilty to everything, but he had to do a full disclosure during his sentencing and that's what I wanted to be there for. I needed to hear him say what he had done and hopefully I would be able to understand why. I sat in that courtroom with my family and listened to this nigga give a full disclosure that shocked me so many different times.

I listen to him tell how he actually was sitting on the sofa and watched the robbery/execution of Sean, Jackie's brother. He told how he set BJ up to get back at me. He told how they did a bunch of bullshit lying to get Jackie out of jail and even gave the name of the attorney who helped him….. Tia. I just shook my head in pure disgust that not only was he telling on himself but snitching out other people also. He told how after I kicked them out of Miami when they came down for my wedding, the four of them hatched a plan to kill me and possibly CiCi, Yes, you heard me right. Simm, Jackie, CoCo and Tiff were plotting to kill me and possibly my son. The plan was to kidnap CiCi and hold him for ransom and when I showed to pay for his safe return because that was one of the conditions, they would kill us both. I didn't want to believe that Jackie or my sister and cousin would conspire to kill me and my child but when Simm disclosed that was the reason he finally killed all three of them… because they went back on their word I felt it was true.

The tears started falling as I listened to this man tell everyone how he lied and slithered in the grass like the snake his ass is to get Jackie out the house and over to CoCo and Tiffs. He had already killed them and he told Jackie he needed his help to get rid of the bodies... but he instead killed him also and put the three of them together for show and then skipped town. He planned to come back and kill me another time but the demons of his past begin to haunt him and he just couldn't take it anymore. The judge sentenced him to life in prison without the possibility of parole.

He asked to address the court before he was taken away and I thought he would apologize to Maxine, and Jill who were both in attendance for taking the lives of their children for absolutely nothing. Instead this nigga looked at me and told me it was all my fault. If I had just stopped being a bitch and realized all he had done for me and fucking married him, nobody would have had to die. I knew then that Simm was out his fucking mind. The day after Simm made his disclosure that mentioned Tia's dirty dealings, she found herself in hot water... and by the end of the week, somehow or another Simm hung himself on a doorknob in the prison library.... Yeah right. Ian had that nigga touched and I knew it was gonna happen the minute he mentioned Tia in his bullshit.

The day after Simm was sentenced, before I boarded my plane and headed home to the peaceful life I had come to enjoy with Fred down in Texas, I had the driver who picked me up from the hotel take me for one last spin around the city. I sat in the back of the Suburban and watched the sights and sounds of DC pass by from behind the tint of the windows. We rode down H Street NE, and while shit was changing majorly due to gentrification I still held mad memories. I remember coming down here with Dana to do my back to school shopping as a child. As we made it on to Benning Road, I took in the sight of Hecinger Mall and remembered wearing the payphones out up there, I remembered eating from China House carryout aka THE RAT which sat across the street. We rode down 17th street and even the Rec, and the field were now different. As the driver turned on to E Street, my eyes began to tear up. It was nostalgic as I looked upon the building I used to call home. All the memories from the day I met Ciaira, The spot I was sitting in when I first saw Fred. The yard my child and Monae's kids played in as I tried to tell my girls this city and this game was ours for the taking. As I sat there and took it all in, and watched all these new faces occupy the space that once was mine. I realized that I had won.

I played the game of chest and made it to be the last person standing on the board. Now it was time for new Queens, Kings and Pawns to take the stage. As the driver rounded the corner of 16th and E and headed for the highway to get me to the airport, I knew that would be my last trip to DC. I had everything I wanted and needed…. All that really mattered to me was down in Texas waiting on my safe return. As we came out of the third street tunnel taking the exit headed to Virginia, I chucked the deuces to the place that made me. With no regrets, I adjusted my shades and sat back and smiled.

So many motherfuckas spent their years hustling to be seen…. This bitch here hustled to disappear, and that's exactly what I was doing.

The Queen Had Left The Building.

From The Desk Of K Sherrie

Ten years ago when I wrote this series, I honestly had no idea how high I would fly one day on the wings of Keeli, Ciaira, Monae and Kia. This has been an amazing start to my journey as an author. When I released this series, to say I was scared is a gross understatement. As a writer, I won't lie, I'm a fickle human being and yes can be sensitive about the people who live in my head. I was so unsure of how people would receive my folks, my writing, just me period and I have to say in hindsight, I was tripping. The response to my girls was overwhelming. Nothing of what I expected. Each and every time I encounter someone who is reading my work for the first time or the 5th time, the feeling I get is indescribable. I'm not big on acknowledgements, I honestly don't read them in other people's books because well at first I honestly didn't understand it. It wasn't until I sat down to prepare this final installment of this series and reflected on this journey that the importance of the acknowledgement set in and I felt the duty to write them. And I will be honest, right now there are sooooooo many different names floating through my head that writing them all would be a book in itself. So please don't take it personal that I am NOT gonna go word for word, line for line, person for person. Not that it's not important but maaaaaannnnn, that shit takes time and I know y'all would rather me be busy writing than saying HEEEEEEEEYYYYY GIRL to everybody. So, I will say thank you to every reader who has picked up a copy of this series and allowed the people in my head to take you on a journey. Thank you to everybody who ever took the time to leave a review that was REAL and what you really felt after reading my work. Thank you to every author in this game who accepted me as a peer, and a huge shout out to the ones who have taken the time to add me to your list of folks you just gotta read. That means so much to me. Thank you to everyone who has sent a word of encouragement, an inbox just to talk about what I wrote, thank you to the people who I initially met as readers and now I am proud to call friends.

Shout out and a huge thank you to the book club DIVERSIFIED READERS. I was soooo geeked when Mia sent me the message and let me know y'all were reading this series and invited me to the meeting. I was soooo nervous because that was my first sit down but y'all crazy asses kept me ROLLING and I 100% appreciate the local love and support. Y'all rock!

Shout out and huge thanks to my three favorite online/facebook book clubs SiRR (Sisters into Reading and Reviewing) and   My Urban Book Clubs The connections I have made within these three groups have been priceless. So thank you to all 50/11 million members for your support be it with reading my work, or just your day to day conversation etc and a super huge thank you to Denise and Brandie, creating these spaces and all you ladies do to support authors old and new to this game.

A special thank you to what I like to call my home team. My fiancé, and our son. Like I said I wrote this series 10 whole years ago and it just sat in my computer doing nothing because I had let life and all of its woes I faced back then beat the confidence and the fight out of me. But you two, you were the reason I gained my fire back. The reason I was able to stop being afraid and take a chance on myself. You two are the reason I strive daily to be a better person. Without you, I'd be lost in this world… thank you both for being in my corner and being the best Future husband and son a girl could ask for. Love you both to infinity and beyond 10 times!

And MY MAMA OOOOOOOOOOOOOOOHHHHHHHHHHHHHH I LOVE YOU! (LLS)

Word to J. Cole, I NEED to thank my loving mother, who sadly it took me sooo many years to see that all you've ever wanted for me was the best and that's why you were so hard on me. I get asked a lot if Dana, the mother in this series is based on you. So I have to explain a lot that Dana is the mother I THOUGHT I wanted and needed back in the day. The mother who let me run the show. In hindsight, I realize how much of a fool I truly was. I thank you for never giving up on me, even when I know me and my antics drove you so close to the edge. Even now, as an adult, I thank you for always being my mother…. And never ever caring if I like you or not. HA!

Thanking God goes without saying because without him, I wouldn't even be sitting here right now typing any of this. I am so thankful that through it all he has kept me here and I feel it's for this very reason because I could've been gone a loooong time ago. So I will continue to scream his praises.

Lastly, I have to say thank you to a very special group of ladies who I miss dearly daily. Angie, Angel, CiCi, Letha, Tiff-Bama, Kori, Alicia, Kortney, Veta, Tab, Tiff J and Bianca. Each day that I spend on this journey, I think back to the friendship we once shared and I hate that I am not able to share this experience with you all because it would have been fucking EPIC. I know it's nobody to blame for that but myself but I still want to let y'all know that I miss y'all and love y'all

all sincerely despite the bullshit. Love is something I don't believe you can fake and in my heart y'all will always be my sisters. Thank you all for helping me through some of the toughest moments of my life. Sincerely, without y'all who knows where I would be. Love you untidy bitches to the moon and back!

That's all I got. Again thank you all for all your support and love and I hope y'all ready because BAYBEEEEEEEEEEEE this is ONLY the beginning. Check y'all in the next book,

I Am K Sherrie

Be sure to finish out this series by checking out the other side of the game in these two bangers....

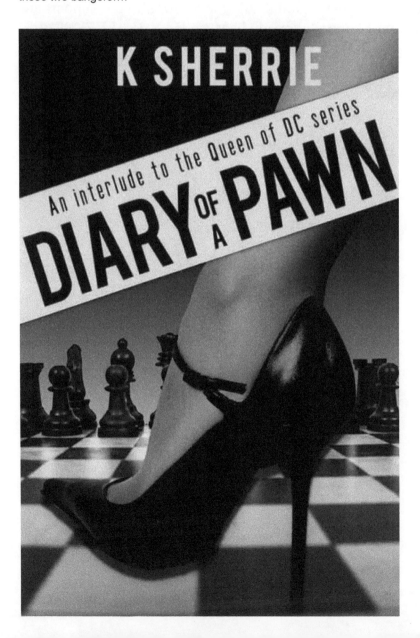

The pawn is the most numerous piece in the game, and in most circumstances, also the weakest.

While they started out as lovers, family and friends, their actions along the way to Keeli Byrd's success made them expendable gaining them the title as pawns. But being that life is full circle the same people you step on going up are sometimes the same ones who grab your ankles and snatch you down.

Simm

Jackie

Monae

Kia

They are all back and gearing up for the grand finale....... The Story Of Her Demise.